Dazed

Rose of Petrichoria

Prequel

By Katie Hauenstein

For my daughter,
whose burgeoning desire to learn to read
inspires me to write.

Table of Contents

Prologue
10 Years Before *Forgotten*

On July seventh, a day the world will never forget, I stood with Father and Mother on the balcony at the front of Evergreen Palace. Our flag, brown with a green evergreen arched by twelve ivory stars, flapped in the gentle summer breeze. The courtyard was filled with people. In fact, the city streets were full, as well. Even though I couldn't see the roads and alleys from where I was, I knew people from all over Arboria, wearing black, crowded the roads to be together on this occasion.

It was the Memorial Day of the Dazed. The day Oramatosis was released to the public. It was a day we remembered the cost of one man selfishly giving into the temptation for more power. His surrender to temptation led to our ancestors' minds being altered, and to the ruin of the world we had to rebuild from scratch.

Father was speaking, reminding us all that we must always be diligent to be conscious of our minds at all times. Temptation comes at unexpected times and if we do not stop it, it can ruin our lives and the lives of those around us. I shook my head sadly. All those people were dead because of it.

When presented with the vaccine cure to prevent the infection of Oramatosis, there were some people who were too prideful or too scared to take it. They are dead now, also.

A tear slid down my cheek. It was two hundred years ago. No matter how much time passes, I don't think I will ever be able to spend the Memorial Day of the Dazed without a shed tear or two, even if I wasn't there when it happened.

"We will now begin our day of silence," Father said. It would be the last thing spoken in our kingdom that day. All over the world, people were having similar services and at some point early in the morning, every leader would say the same words in their own languages. All over the world, there would be silence for remembrance.

In Arboria, we took it a step further. With the silence, we also spent the day in solitude and fasting. We remembered how alone the Dazed were, and that a good number of them starved to death in their insanity.

We *had* to remember. We *could* not let it happen again. If I had anything to say or do about it, it *would* not happen again.

A big part of my training growing up was to restrain myself when temptation of any kind presented itself to me. I was successful, overall, but I was only human. Peter was my downfall. I wasn't supposed to fall in love, but I did, and he loved me in return.

Everyone silently emptied the streets and went to their rooms. Whether it was a hotel room or a personal room, today everyone would spend it the same way: alone and reflecting on the temptations that come across us as individuals every day.

When I made it back to my room at the top of Evergreen Palace, I laid down on my overstuffed sofa. I didn't bother changing out of my dress. My assistant had the day off and I was proud that I was able to get the corset on all by myself. I didn't want to undo that work quite yet.

I sighed.

Pride.

Standing up, I unzipped the flowy black dress that was made especially for today and began making work of the darned corset. My fingers were still sore from working at putting it *on,* and taking it *off* certainly was not helping.

I hope my fingers don't bleed.

The hope was in vain, though. About midway through unlatching the corset, I felt a prick of blood on my right ring finger. Rather than stop me, it just made me move quicker, wanting to get it over with.

At least the dress is black...

Finally, I finished and carefully peeled the corset and dress all the way off. Before touching any other clothing, I walked into my bathroom and turned on the faucet. Hissing, I put my hands under the clear water, which turned pink as the blood from multiple fingertips mingled with it.

After shutting off the faucet, I opened a drawer and pulled out my small cut weaver and traced it along my fingertips, quickly healing the superficial wounds.

Deciding on a short nightgown, I put it on and laid back on the sofa again. Temptation.

What temptations always plague me? Pride. Discontent. Anger. Peter.

Oddly enough, the desire for more power had never been a temptation of mine. In fact, I would gladly give up my place as heir to the Crown for the chance to live a normal life. In less than a month's time, my seven suitors would be presented to me. One was Peter, but there was no guarantee Father would choose him.

Closing my eyes, I prayed for wisdom, patience, and contentment in my circumstances. I prayed that my kingdom would never see a time as dark as the time when the world was overrun with the insanity of the Daze.

Part I

Chapter 1

"Why? Why did I have to be born during the hottest time of the year?" I complained as I awaited entry to the ballroom. Tugging at the bottom of my right sleeve, I continued my whining. "Seriously. That and corsets and – why am I wearing long sleeves? Who picked this dress, anyway?"

"You did," responded my exasperated cousin, Ella. "You said the sleeves were lovely and you liked the way they belled out."

"Well – it was a dumb idea." The dress *was* lovely, but incredibly uncomfortable in the heat. The emerald green color brought out the deep green of my eyes. Having a square neck, it allowed full view of my long, black hair laying in soft, unnatural, curls against my pale skin. Normally, my hair was stick straight, but I had my assistant put some curls in it for the evening's event.

"I tried to tell you that, but you wouldn't listen."

I turned and gave her a dirty look and puckered my lips. She was smiling and it was so big, it extended up to her sparkling blue eyes. "I see you find my predicament funny," I noted.

"A little." She began to laugh at that, causing her tight, blonde curls to bounce. A short reflection of my protest made me realize how ridiculous I was being and I rolled my eyes with a laugh, too.

"You're right. I am standing in a palace grumbling about a ball gown. Princess Problems." We laughed harder.

When I was going on about an issue I only had because I was being a frilly Princess, one of us would claim "Princess Problems" and pull me back to earth. Not that people in my kingdom were suffering by any means.

Indeed, Arboria was in its prime. Our exportation of lumber and fruits, found only in our part of the world anymore, was on the rise. The people were happy and we were getting ready to enter into an exciting event. Well, it was exciting for everyone but me.

"Are you nervous?" Ella asked, pulling me from my thoughts.

"What kind of question is that? Of course I'm nervous!" I replied incredulously.

Ella looked down to her folded hands. "I'm sorry. It was a dumb question. I do not envy you having to do this. There are many benefits to being the Princess of Arboria, but this is not one of them."

I nodded. "Not everything is imported silks and chocolates. Despite the beautiful home and fancy things, there are still sacrifices to be made."

We moved forward as Father and Mother made their entrance. Ella put a hand on my shoulder. "It worked out for Uncle Aaron, Rose. It could work out for you."

"Seventy-five percent." I said with gritted teeth. I was repeating the statistic of successful results for this particular tradition I had memorized and had ungraciously been reminding anyone who said anything like Ella had to me. Father always replied with something about success being relative, while Mother would scowl at me and remind me that happiness wasn't a requirement of being Queen. I didn't expect her to understand. She had benefited greatly from the arrangement and they *did* have success with happiness.

Ella knew better than to take it any further. Having her by my side meant the world to me. It was a declaration of her commitment to help me through everything in the coming months. Her entrance would be her declaration of accepting the position of Crown Princess' Maiden – and it was her time to go in.

She squeezed my shoulder one last time and released me as she went into the room. Lucky lady. This was the closest she would ever come to having to participate in anything remotely like the King's Test. In a month and two days, it would begin for me. In around four months and two days, it would be over and six of seven eligible young noblemen would be available for Ella to choose from.

As I waited for my turn to go in, I tried to convince myself that the process wasn't medieval. It was my duty and it was an honor.

An honor. Right. What an honor to spend three months with men competing for me like I am some kind of prize.

Though I knew the history of the Test, I still did not understand how the first King of Arboria could have possibly found it to be the most reasonable route for his daughter to marry. Maybe she fell in love with a loser – or a commoner. I tapped the toe of my shoe on the hardwood floor.

Would it be so wrong to fall in love with a commoner?

Because I would never get the opportunity to marry for love at all, much less with a commoner, the question was irrelevant. I knew from the gossip shows on the holocomm and fan columns in the Daily Net that the men of the kingdom found me beautiful. They would probably kill for the chance to marry me; there probably would have been an uprising if the original plan for foreigners to participate in this generation's King's Test went through.

The doors to the ballroom opening alerted me to my time of entrance. When I came in, the herald announced me. "Her Royal Highness, Princess Miriam Petrichoria of Arboria!" As I descended the steps, I took in the sight of the line of seven men before me. All were handsome; three I barely knew, two were identical twins whom I had known since childhood, one was my best friend, and one was my true love – a true love I should not have.

I smiled demurely when I stopped at the end of the stairs and waited for the herald to continue. "Men of this generation's King's Test, please step forward as I introduce you to the Princess." At this, each man began to discreetly preen. Some stood straighter and puffed out their chests, some dropped folded hands to sides, some rearranged their feet, and some did all of those things plus shake their heads to make sure their hair was just right.

"Count Brian of Birch!" The herald announced. The first gentleman in line stepped forward. He was short, but not shorter than me, and stocky with bright blue eyes and military cropped blond hair. I didn't know him well, but knew he was accomplished in the Royal Arborian Guard. "Princess Miriam, I look forward to getting to know you better over the next few months," he said politely as he took my hand and kissed it, then stepped back in line. All of that was done without a hint of a smile.

Ha! He doesn't want to be here any more than I do. I wonder if he already loves someone else, too.

"Count Christopher of Alder!" The herald continued and the man every girl in the kingdom, besides me, deemed the most handsome stepped forward. "I think we will make an excellent match, Princess Miriam," he said with a cocky smile plastered on his fake-tanned face. He bent into a bow, keeping his dark eyes glued to mine, and kissed my hand, then stepped back.

No, we won't, Mr. Confident. If I have anything to do with it, you'll be the first to go.

See, that was the problem. Not all the noblemen were jerks, but more than half of them were, as far as I could tell.

"Count Leonard of Elm!" The older twin, by seconds, stepped forward. He kept his bright orange hair ear length and his bangs were always in his sea-green eyes, creating a sort of tick in which he flung his head back to the right to keep them out. He believed he was God's gift to women. Granted, he *was* good-looking, but a woman needs much more than a handsome face to make her happy. "I know we will make a great pair, Princess Miriam," he said when he bowed and kissed my hand, then stepped back.

What a shame they can't hear each other. How original.

"Count Lincoln of Elm!" The younger twin, with buzzed red hair and the same green eyes, stepped forward. While his brother believed he was God's gift to women, Lincoln knew he was God's gift to the world. "I promise to rule justly and fairly with you, Princess Miriam," he said as he bowed and stepped back.

No kiss? At least I know his end game. This is a path to the Crown, not my heart for this one.

"Count Peter of Juniper!" My love stepped forward. He was taller than me by a half foot with chocolate brown eyes, short blonde hair, and he was strong enough to literally sweep me off my feet. With a giant grin, he said, "I will do my best, Rose," as he bowed, kissed my hand, then stepped back.

I hope your best is good enough, Peter.

It was no secret that Peter wasn't the brightest lightening in a stormy sky, but he was a good man, charming, and he loved me.

"Count Stephan of Oak!" Up stepped a man who was like a brother to me. He was tall and deceptively lanky, with nearly tip-of-ears length, light brown hair and grey-green eyes. He smiled warmly at me and looked at me with what appeared to be true adoration in his eyes. "This should be fun, Rose." He bowed, kissed my hand, and then stepped back.

What was that look about?

"Count Theodore of Willow!" My favorite dance partner. He was about the same height as Peter, but kept his black hair long and

11

pulled back in a low ponytail at the nape of his neck. He held my gaze with his brown eyes, which were shining with a glint of humor. I had no idea what he was thinking, but whatever it was amused him. "I look forward to knowing you in a setting besides the dance floor. You will be dancing with me tonight, yes?" he said as he bowed, kissed my hand, awaited my answering nod, then stepped back.

Of course we are. I have to dance with all of you once.

"Ladies and gentlemen! The men of this generation's King's Test!" the herald declared. The room erupted in applause and shouts of jubilation. "Now, Princess Miriam will choose her partner for dancing The Rose to officially begin our evening of celebration!"

Chapter 2

Of course, I already knew who my dance partner would be. Everyone else probably knew, as well. I always began balls with Peter now, much to Theo's chagrin. Seeing as though it was a special occasion, however, I decided to at least pretend to think about it.

I made a scene of beginning at the end of the line with Theo and strolling thoughtfully to the other, making eye contact with each man. When I turned around to make my way back, I stopped at Leonard and teased him by raising my brow at him. When he put a stupid grin on his face, I continued on and the room laughed. Finally, I stopped at Peter and gave him my hand.

He smiled and I mirrored the smile back to him. As we walked to the center of the dance floor, the crowd parted and formed a circle around us. The music began and we danced effortlessly to the song in three quarter time in companionable silence. Being in his arms was like basking in rays of sunshine after a few months of endless rain and overcast sky. I never wanted it to end. Mainly because I knew when it did, I would begin a rotation through the participants of the King's Test as dance partners for the rest of the evening.

The song ended and, as expected, when Peter bowed out, Brian stepped in.

At least I'll get an extra dance with Peter tonight.

Brian bowed, I curtseyed, and he slowly moved to take my hand and waist. A moment later, the dance began. Fortunately, because each participant was guaranteed a dance and a private conversation during the King's Test Ball, all the music would be slow, so I wouldn't become exhausted. Unfortunately, this meant each man would hold me close and I would be forced to talk to them all as we glided across the dance floor.

Brian stayed quiet for the first half of the song and had a hard time keeping eye contact with me. Just when I was thinking it might not be so bad after all, he opened his mouth and looked me in the eyes.

"You are beautiful this evening, Princess Miriam. I have always liked that color green on you. It brings out the color in your eyes."

"Um. Thank you, Count Brian. We will be together a lot in the coming months. You can just call me Miriam, if you would like."

He gave me a crooked smile and I could feel his arms loosen up a bit. "You can call me Brian, Miriam."

It appeared as though my initial thought that he didn't want to be there was wrong; he was just nervous. Trying not to tense up, I skipped a beat and almost fell. With quick reflexes he had developed through years of combat training, he caught me and managed to make it look like it was all a part of the dance.

"Thank you, Brian." I smiled at him.

"Have you heard about my recent promotion? I am third in command now," he boasted without acknowledging my gratitude.

"Yes, I have. Congratulations. It is quite an honor for one so young to become the Lieutenant General of our military."

He must have been pleased with the compliment because he pulled me a little closer to him. "If things go well for me with the King's Test, I will become the Commander in Chief. I am far more qualified than anyone else participating for that title."

14

And there it is. One wants only to be King. One is only interested in becoming the leader of our military.

Tilting my head like a curious cat, I said, "You know, there is far more to being the King than leading the military."

His eyes widened. "Of – of course. I am qualified in other areas as well."

"There is more to being King than being King, as well."

He furrowed his brow. "I do not understand."

"Hmm." That was all I said as the song ended. I figured it would give him some time to consider the fact that being King of Arboria would also make him my husband. When he walked away, baffled, Count Christopher, Arboria's Most Desired, approached and looked at me seductively with his dark blue eyes.

I hope this is a short song.

I thought this, despite knowing that the songs would all be pretty much the same length to keep things fair among the participants. We wouldn't want anyone becoming jealous. There was no hesitation with Christopher like there was with Brian. He also didn't hesitate to immediately drop the "Princess" when talking with me, even though we were nowhere near friendly enough to ignore formality without my permission. Pressing me against himself, he began talking.

"Miriam, I am delighted to get the chance to hold you in my arms tonight. So often, Peter, Stephan, and Theo take up all your dance time at these events."

"Yes. Well. To be fair, this is the first and only ball of this kind," I retorted, annoyed that I had never noticed him watching me in the past.

He grinned like a shark. "Touché. But I am sure you know what I mean."

15

"Yes. Though you have never seemed to be lacking as far as dance partners go. There are always a few ladies disappointed from not being able to dance with you by the end of a ball."

He quirked a brow. "You have noticed me dancing with other women?"

"You say 'other women' as if I have some claim on you."

"You just might at the end of the King's Test."

"You seem rather confident in yourself."

He shrugged. "I have been studying. And the women of Arboria love me."

I laughed at that. "Studying? What could you possibly be studying? *I* do not even know what this generation's King's Test entails."

He bent forward until his lips almost touched my ear. "You." When he brought his face away from my ear, he kept himself within inches of my face.

"Oh. You are *good*." The song ended and I pulled his ear down to my lips and whispered, "Does that ever *actually* work?"

He walked away dumbstruck as Leonard came for his turn around the room with me. Getting ready for round two of Arboria's Most Desired, I curtseyed. When Leonard came up from his bow, he threw his head back to the right to get his bangs off his face and I winced inwardly. His tick had always driven me crazy. Like Christopher, he pulled me flush against him. He looked at me with heat in his gaze and I tried desperately not to laugh.

"Princess Miriam, you are lovely tonight, as you always are."

"Thank you, Count Leonard. Please, we have known each other so long and our parents are good friends. You do not need to use my title."

He pursed his lips. He must have thought I would let him use the name my family and friends called me, Rose. Though, he was able to quickly recover and smile. "And you can call me Leo, Miriam."

I glanced around the ballroom and noted that Christopher had made a quick recovery as well; he already had a woman swooning in his arms on the dance floor. When I looked back at Leo, he was still looking at me intently. From then on, I tried to make a point of being a good dance partner by keeping eye contact.

"Our parents *have* been good friends for quite a few years, have they not?" he asked.

"Indeed."

"You know, our mothers both competed in our parents' generation's Queen's Test."

"Yes, they did. It is so nice they were able to become friends out of it."

"Hmm. Perhaps it is meant to be, then."

"What is that, Leo?"

He lowered his hand from the middle of my back to my lower back – my *very* lower back; his bending caused his hair to fall over his eye. "You and me." Tick. "I think we make a good match." Tick.

"You know, in the twenty first century, they had this product called hairspray. It was meant to hold hair in place."

"Alright," he drawled. That's when I realized he was completely oblivious to his tick. "Do you always bring up random historical facts when you are nervous?"

I smiled. "I am not nervous, Leo. Just out of curiosity, though," I started as the song ended. "You realize the same logic you just presented could be used for your brother as well, right?"

17

He walked away, bemused, as his brother, Lincoln, approached. Unlike his lecherous brother, Lincoln danced at a proper distance, but not so distant that he seemed uninterested. While we weren't close friends, he and I had always gotten along better than I had with his brother. However, they both had a generous amount of ego in their personalities that simply burst every time they were with me.

As the song began, he said, "I am sorry for my brother, Princess. I am afraid he has been fond of you for many years and has not picked up on how to be a gentleman. It was totally inappropriate for him to put his hand – there."

I laughed. "It is quite alright, Count Lincoln. I have dealt with men worse than that before. No need to call me 'Princess,' by the way. Our mothers are friends. I think we can drop that formality."

He nodded. "Please, call me 'Linc,' then, Miriam. Please do not tell me that he presented you with the logic that he is your most logical choice because our mother competed against your mother in their generation's Queen's Test."

I nodded with a tight, amused smile at how well Linc knew his twin. "He did, indeed – near the end of the song. I, then, informed him I could use the same logic for you if it was good enough cause for a decision."

Linc laughed. "Is *that* why he walked away like a kicked puppy?"

"I think so, yes." *Maybe he's not so bad.* "You know, I do not think I have ever spent any time with you separate from Leo."

"No, you have not. But that is alright. We will have plenty of time to get to know each other as individuals soon enough. I am excited to prove myself worthy of the Crown."

Then again, maybe he is.

"I have been training with Brian in strategy and combat and I have worked closely with my father on dealings with the people and administration."

"I am surprised Brian would train you at all. He seems quite competitive. Are you sure his training is trustworthy?"

"Of course. We have come to an agreement."

Raising a brow and tilting my head, I asked a question I wasn't sure I wanted the answer to. "And what is that, Linc?"

"Should I become King, he will get a promotion to High General. Should he win, I will."

"How can you get a promotion? You are not even in the Royal Arborian Guard. And what would happen to High General Miller?"

Linc shrugged. "It does not matter. As King, you can appoint anyone as your second in command. If it was me, I would give High General Miller a great retirement."

The song was ended. "I will tell you what I told Brian, Linc. There is more to being King than being King." Unsurprisingly, he gave me the same look Brian had when he walked away. Peter came and held me just right as the song began. Not as close as Lecherous Leo and not as far as Boring Brian.

"You are absolutely stunning tonight, Rose. All I want to do is sneak you away to our normal spot and kiss you senseless."

I laughed. "Unfortunately, it's not going to be possible tonight. I have to dance with all these men. At least I get an extra dance with you, and Stephan and Theo are good dance partners."

It was nice to relax a little. With Peter and Stephan, I wouldn't have to be so formal and it was a nice break from my previous dance encounters.

"I felt like ripping Leo's hand off when he brought it so close to your – "

19

"Don't worry about it, Peter. It's alright," I said, gently tapping his back with my hand to try to calm his barely-contained rage.

"It's *not* alright, Rose. How many times are you going to be molested by Christopher and Leo over the next few months?"

"I don't know, but at least you don't have to worry about Brian or Linc. They are both utterly confused. I ended both their dances by telling them, 'There's more to being King than being King.' Pretty sure Brian is killing brain cells trying to figure it out over there." I nonchalantly tilted my head over in Brian's direction where he was leaning against the wall deep in thought and Peter laughed.

"Blossoms, Rose. I wish I didn't have to compete for your heart."

"You don't. You just need to compete for the Crown. You already won my heart years ago."

"If I win, I can't wait until I can kiss you publically and declare from the top of Evergreen Palace's largest tree that you're mine."

"I have faith in you, Peter. It's *when* not *if*."

"You're probably the only one – well, besides Father and Mother, but they don't count."

"You're ridiculous."

"No, really." The song was nearing the end. "Pay attention to everyone when Stephan approaches you. *He's* the favorite."

"Do I detect jealousy? Peter, you know Stephan is only a friend to me – well, a brother."

"To *you*, yes." Peter kissed my hand as he left the floor at the end of the song. I did as he asked and casually glanced around the room as Stephan approached. Everyone stopped talking one by one and pretty soon there was applause – *actual* applause! Stephan's face turned bright red and he gave a polite wave to the crowd. I was surprised when he pulled me against himself and he looked assertively into my eyes.

As the music began, I said, "Roots! Looks like we all know who the favorite is." People knew Peter and I were friends, but it was common knowledge that Stephan and I were childhood *best* friends – aside from Ella, of course. I figured the combination between Stephan's competence and a romantic notion of childhood friends falling in love had something to do with their favor of him.

Stephan chuckled and shook his head. "It's not a gameshow, Rose. It doesn't matter who the favorite is. Are you doing alright? I've noticed a few of these men getting awfully fresh with you."

"*Fresh*? Have you been looking into twenty and twenty-first century terminology?"

He smiled and shrugged. "I wanted to see what was so fascinating about the time period for you." His face grew serious. "Seriously, though. Are you alright?"

"I'm fine, Stephan. I'm a big girl. I can handle myself."

"A woman is never fine if she says 'I'm fine' like that. But I'll let it go. You do seem to be handling yourself quite well. Peter is the only one so far who has left the dance floor not looking defeated. Are you going to defeat me?"

"Oh. I don't think that's possible, Stephan. You're carrying yourself with a level of assurance I haven't seen before."

"In me?"

"In anyone, really."

After a pause, he pulled me a little closer and said, "Would this be so horrible, Rose?"

I tilted my head. "Would *what* be so horrible?"

"This? You and me ruling together? *Being* together? I know you're having a hard time with all this. I truly understand. It's not fair to have such an important decision taken from you, but – it wouldn't be so bad if it was me, right? You know I would take care of you."

I smiled. "I know. It wouldn't be bad at all if it was you."

It wasn't until I heard another round of applause that I realized the song was over. Stephan hadn't let go yet and we were so deep in conversation, I wasn't even paying attention to the music. That was one of the main reasons he was my best friend. He was always concerned for me and when we talked, it was as if no one and nothing else mattered.

Stephan kissed my hand and passed it over to Theo, who was patiently waiting. Perfect dancer that he was, he held me at the same distance Peter did. Honestly, while he was my favorite dance partner, I didn't know much about him at all. His parents were older and he was the youngest in his household – that was the extent of my knowledge.

"Last dance," he said with a smirk. "Let us make it a good one."

I laughed. He *did* have a gorgeous smile. We began to move to the rhythm of the music and everyone watched, as mesmerized by Theo's talent as I was.

"What do you think, Princess? Does an old man like me even stand a chance?" While he was the youngest in his household, he was the oldest of the King's Test participants. He sat at the top of the age qualifications at twenty-six.

I smiled warmly at him. "I hardly think it would be fair of me to judge your chances based on fancy footwork, Count Theo."

He feigned disappointment in his gaze. "Oh! But if you did, certainly I would be King of Arboria *and* your heart. And please, call me Theo."

"Miriam. You have some smooth words there, Theo."

"All the better to make declarations and whisper sweet nothings with, my dear."

Theo and I had always had fun together on the dance floor, but he had never been so flirtatious with me. It made sense that he would be now, though. He had probably been classically trained in dance – and flirtation – just so he could literally sweep me off my feet.

"Are you a wolf, Theo? Should I be afraid and hide all my red cloaks?"

He growled with laughter, and I squealed with glee, as he lifted me by the waist and spun in a circle, causing the crowd to applaud. As we swept passed Christopher and Leo, I could hear them audibly groan.

"Oh, please do not. Red is a most lovely color on you." His smile faded and he began to simplify the dance so he could speak more seriously to me. I was breathless, though the rhythm was slow, the banter and steps had tired me a bit. It was only then that I realized he had drawn me closer to him.

"Miriam, you are the most beautiful woman I know – that I have ever known. While I jest about my dancing being reason enough to be King of this glorious kingdom and holder of your heart, I do hope to prove myself to you in the coming months."

The music ended, he kissed my hand, and stepped back into the line of gentlemen I had not realized had formed again.

Now here comes the longest part of the evening. Short interviews with each one with no music to interrupt.

I sighed as Ella walked up to me and we made our way to the center of my rose garden.

23

Chapter 3

"Are you nervous?" Ella asked me again.

"What kind of a question is that? 'Are you nervous?' No, Ella. I'm positively giddy at the prospect of being alone with seven men who I know will kiss me at some point. This is the second time you have asked me that silly question tonight."

Ella laughed. "You're so cute when you're nervous."

I smirked. "Shut up, Ella."

We walked through the maze and I sat on my sofa swing, glad I had not chosen a huge dress. True, the only person I had ever been romantic with was Peter, but I felt most comfortable here, in my garden. The whole point of the evening was to introduce each man to a part of me personally. It hadn't always been a ball for previous generations. The introduction was the only part of the Test that the heir had a say in. Father, for example, had chosen a beautiful hike and picnic for his Queen's Test Introduction. His private interviews/first kisses were done in a little grove not far from the end of the hike.

My love of dancing and roses was no secret to anyone, so it was not a big surprise how I had chosen to spend the evening. Peter wasn't very happy with the prospect of sharing our private spot, but he knew it would seem strange if I didn't use it.

25

My Crown Princess' Maiden stood dutifully and allowed me a moment to gather myself back together. After taking a few deep breaths and shaking out my hands, I gave Ella a nod and she walked down the glass hallway to let Brian in.

Part of this interview involved the gentleman finding his way through the maze, without being informed that he was going to do a maze. I fully anticipated Brian to make it the fastest, besides Peter, of course, especially after all his bragging earlier in the evening about his military prowess.

I heard his footsteps down the hallway, then the abrupt stop at the entrance. While everyone knew I had a personal rose garden, admittance was solely at my discretion. Not many had been there.

"Miriam?" Brian's hesitant baritone called out.

"I am here."

I hate using formal speech. It feels so unnatural.

"Where?"

"You are the Lieutenant General. Let us see how long it takes you to find me." I tried to sound playful even though I was secretly hoping he would waste most of his time trying to find his way to me.

However, I was disappointed to find that he was truly as resourceful as he said he was. Rather than try to find his way *through* the maze, he climbed the stone wall and leapt from wall to wall until he found where I was in the center. Nimbly, he jumped down, making sure to bend his knees when he landed, and gave me a smug grin.

"Clever." I said and shook my head with a smile.

"I told you I was good with military strategy," Brian said as he swaggered over to my sofa swing and grabbed the bar over my head. "What good would I be if I could not figure out a simple garden maze?"

A little stunned by his new-found self-certainty, I looked up at his face, which was now towering over me. "Is that what this is to you? Strategy?"

He shrugged and I noticed his biceps bulge a bit beneath his Royal Arborian Guard dress jacket. "Are you stifling warm in that jacket, Brian?"

He laughed dryly. "Yes, very." But he left it on and sat next to me on the bench and took my hand. Taken aback again, I looked at him to see he was close and trying desperately to meet my gaze. I obliged. "I have been thinking about what you said earlier all evening, Miriam."

I swallowed. I knew he was going to kiss me at some point. Not knowing when was making me a nervous wreck.

It's not a big deal. It's just a kiss. Just one. Peter will be here in a while.

"What I said?" I asked innocently.

He gave me a crooked grin. "Yes. 'There is more to being King than being King.' Remember?"

I blinked. "Yes."

"You are right. I am a bit of an idiot." I laughed and he relaxed a little. "I have been approaching this all wrong. I wish I could blame my parents – they spent my whole life engraining how important the military is – but I am twenty-four now and am responsible for my own thoughts and actions. The King's Test is more than a job interview." He ran his index finger from my temple to my chin.

"It was totally thoughtless of me to forget that this is about your life as much as the future King's, whoever it ends up being. I do not confess to be the most romantic man in the world; I know I am not the most attractive. However, if I do end up making it to the end, I want you to know that I will live every day trying to be a man you deserve."

27

That's when he did it. He kissed me. It was a good line. Unsurprisingly, his kiss was hard and commanding. He held me tightly against him and groaned as he deepened the kiss, which I *was* surprised was even possible. It felt like he wanted every inch of me. When he stopped, he held me in an embrace and was shaking. I felt something wet trickle down the side of my head and realized he was weeping.

Breathlessly, I whispered, "Brian, are you crying?"

"I am afraid so." He kissed my cheek and pulled back. "Can I confess something to you?"

"I wish you would."

He wiped his tear from my cheek with a finger. "I have been dreading tonight for months."

"What?"

"It is nothing personal, Miriam. Well, it is, but not the way you are thinking. You are an unbelievably incredible woman. I know you will make a great Queen. Probably one of Arboria's greatest. It is intimidating to know that I not only have to prove myself worthy of the Crown, but of you, too. I hope I can do it. Can you ever forgive my arrogance from earlier?"

"Time's up!" Ella shouted at the entrance. Brian didn't move to leave. He waited for my answer, but I was stupefied by the random exhibition of emotion he just displayed.

"Princess Miriam?" Ella shouted.

"Miriam?" Brian whispered.

"Yes. I can forgive you." I said, stunned.

Brian smiled, got up, and climbed the wall to make his way out of the rose garden.

What just happened? More strategy? No. Those were real tears. Tears! What? I need to stay on my guard.

Chapter 4

"Miiiriaaam?" called Christopher like we were playing a game of hide and seek. I rolled my eyes, even though there was no one to see the expression.

Well, someone *hasn't changed their game plan.*

"I am in the middle of the garden. You will need to find me if you want that first kiss." I teased loudly. He laughed as he entered the maze.

I wondered why it was that this specific, ridiculous ritual was created. Why was it necessary to kiss every single participant before the Test even officially began? Father certainly didn't understand it; why it was necessary and why it was such a big deal to me. "It's just the way it has always been, Rose," he had told me earlier in the day when I was complaining about it again. "I really don't know what the big deal is anyway. It's not like you're being asked to fall in love with seven men. This evening is a demonstration that you are worth more than the Crown. A kiss is personal and can help bring things into perspective for the participants. At least you only have seven; I had twelve at the beginning of my Queen's Test. A set of triplets, even!"

I had cooed in response, "Oh. Poor boy. Father, kisses don't mean as much to a man as they do to a woman. For a woman, she gives love with a kiss. A man just takes possession."

"That is not fair, Rose. And it is not true. I know you don't like some of the men participating, but give them a chance. I'll bet there is more to every man than he shows the public."

That had been the end of it. Perhaps he was right; Brian had shocked me with his emotional kiss.

At some point during my time in my thoughts, I must have closed my eyes. I say this because I was startled when I felt Christopher's body close to mine and the sofa began swinging. Glancing over to him with my one open eye, he said, "Found you. This is a pretty ingenious test, Miriam."

I opened both eyes and turned so I was slightly facing him. "You think I put this together for the King's Test?"

Christopher turned in the same manner. "You did not?"

"No. I mean, I did design it. Years ago. It is my favorite place in Evergreen Palace. You did not learn that in your studies?" I teased.

He blushed. "About that. I am sorry. I am not used to speaking with a woman who is not immediately taken with me."

"So humble!"

Christopher angled a frustrated brow. "Seriously, Miriam. Out of everyone in the kingdom, I would think *you* should understand." His voice held a slight hint of anger. "I mean. Look at you. You know how to play each and every one of us. You know what to say and do to drive us mad with desire."

"Pardon me?" No one had ever talked to me in such a way and I quickly dropped the formality of my speech. "I have no choice here, Christopher. What would you have me do? Treat you all with contempt? Throw a fit about not having a choice who I spend the rest of my life with? Granted, perhaps I could have been kinder with the ones of you who either treated me as if I am a possession or a

Crown, but I am still learning how this Test works, too. I know about as much as you do concerning what comes when the Test begins."

He had barely heard me. "And what is with this expectation of receiving a first kiss from each of us tonight? Now, who is full of herself?"

I stood up and clenched my fists. Shouting, I said, "Are you even hearing me? Do you honestly believe it's my idea to be in each of your arms? To allow you all to kiss me and know me in my most personal place in the palace? To give all my honesty and time to all of you for the next several months? It's not! I wish I didn't have to have a King's Test. I wish I could fall in love with whoever I want as six of the seven of you will be able to do. This isn't necessarily the end for you Christopher. If you don't want me, let me know and I will try to make sure you can go and live your life the way you want."

Turning away, surprised at how hurt I was, I quietly said, "It's the least I could do for both of us."

I heard the swing stop and Christopher stood. I turned back to him. "I know what you mean by not knowing how to be with women when they are not throwing themselves at you. I have had practice. I have good friends who are men, who just think of me as a friend. You haven't had that." He slowly walked closer to me, took my hands in his, and kissed them. "I'm not a self-obsessed, horrid woman, Christopher. I'm just a woman who is terrified I will end up married to someone who doesn't truly love me – and that decision is completely out of my hands."

"I am sorry, Miriam," he whispered. "I had you all wrong. Give me another chance – *choose* to give me another chance. If you do not want to, find a way to be rid of me as soon as you can because I do not want to live the rest of my life without love, either."

I nodded and calmed myself down. "I will give you another chance if you will give me one. I think I made some pretty terrible assumptions about you, too."

He smiled and gently brushed his lips against mine. That was his first kiss for me. He stepped away and left me standing there. Ella didn't even have to come get him when his time was up.

I think Father was right, after all.

Chapter 5

I was still deep in thought when Leo found me in the center. After my experience with Brian and Christopher, I had decided to give him the benefit of the doubt. Our mothers *were* good friends, in any case. He couldn't really be all that bad.

"Hello, Miriam." I looked up to see him standing in the archway leading to the center of my garden.

"Hello, Leo. Look, I am sorry for earlier. I am beginning to realize I have not been handling the situation of the King's Test very well." I took a seat.

He walked over and sat next to me. "Do not worry about it. This must all be very overwhelming for you. Turn around. You are all tense."

I obeyed and turned so my back was facing him. He was right. I was tense and I was always hearing about his back massages from the ladies in Court. Placing his large hands on my shoulders, he began to rub. Involuntarily, my head drooped forward and he laughed.

"I know sometimes I can be a bit of an acquired taste and maybe I was a little forward with you on the dance floor." I chuckled and his hands moved to my upper back. I leaned over so my side was against the sofa, allowing myself complete relaxation.

"A little?" I asked.

"Alright. Maybe a lot forward. Anyway, I have always been unsure of myself with you. Mother has high expectations for Linc and me; she has had them for as long as I can remember." His hands moved to the middle of my back.

"Hmm."

"Truth be told, she is ashamed that neither of us has managed to win your heart yet, with all the time we have spent here growing up."

"That is ridiculous. As if you have any control over my heart. I am sorry you have had to deal with that."

I felt him shrug. "Linc and I have very different strategies when it comes to the King's Test." His hands moved to my lower back, which I didn't realize was sore until he got there. "He feels it will serve him better to prove he is worthy of the Crown." Leo moved his hands around my waist and held me. He whispered in my ear, "I think it will be better to show you how I can benefit you – personally."

He brushed my hair over my shoulder and off my neck and kissed it. I tensed up and turned around. He laughed. "The point is to relax, Miriam." Next thing I knew, he was kissing me. Not hard like Brian and not a brush like Christopher. His kiss was one of passion, like he had been imagining it and perfecting it in his mind his whole life. It felt – wrong. His motive was obvious. This was a play; I was a conquest for him. He kissed me longer than the other two. In fact, he didn't release me until Ella shouted that his time was up. When he did, he placed his fingertips on my swollen lips, then brushed our lips together once more.

Note to self: Sometimes, things are exactly *as they seem.*

Leo left with an annoying strut and Linc pulled the same maneuver Brian had by jumping the walls to the center of the maze.

36

I looked at him with a little humor. "I see Brian *has* been training you."

Linc chuffed. "Why do you say that?"

"Because that is how he got to me, too. Did he tell you to do that?"

He shook his head. "Nope. Those who have been in have not been able to say anything to anybody when they leave. That being said, Leo looked pretty happy with himself."

"I am sure he did," I said without further explanation. If the boys wanted to kiss and tell later, they could.

"Miriam, about my stupidity earlier," he began.

Tired of apologies, I waved him off. "Please, Linc. I cannot take another apology tonight. Let us just forget about it and move on."

He laughed. "Wait. Leo *apologized*?"

I thought about it. "No, I guess he did not. But he should have. I think I need another one from him, too."

Linc rolled his eyes. "Leo, ever believing himself to be a ladies' man."

"You do not think yourself attractive?"

He sat next to me and took my hand. "I do not know. Honestly, it has never seemed all that important to me."

I began to swing the sofa. "Attractiveness in yourself or attractiveness in women."

He narrowed his eyes at me. "There is no right answer there, Miriam."

"Oh, Linc. Always thinking strategy. I really want to know. If there was no Crown and if I were hideous, would you even be remotely interested in me? You have known me longer than some of the other men. You know me well enough to have an opinion."

He looked contemplative for a moment, then said, "Beauty has never been important to me. I think you are beautiful, of course. That cannot be debated. But I think you are prettier inside than out. You are by far the most intelligent woman I know, and you always seem to be fair with the servants around the palace."

I smiled. "You have been considering that assessment of me for some time."

"Yes. I have always had a little childhood crush on you."

I raised my brow at him. "Really? I could never tell."

"Ah. *That* is because I am terribly awkward with women."

I laughed. "So is your brother. He just does not know any better."

At that, he busted out laughing in a way I had never seen from him. He had always been so solemn. All I could do was smile at the sight. When he stopped laughing, he turned to me, eyes sparkling.

Cupping my face gently in his hands, he said, "You are incredible." I closed my eyes, expecting the kiss at any moment, but it didn't come. Slowly, I opened my eyes and saw he was smiling at me. "No."

"No?" I asked, confused.

"No. I will not kiss you tonight."

"But you said –"

"I know what I said." He released my face and brought my fingers to his lips.

"Do you not want to?"

Linc chuckled. "Oh yes. I do. More than anything."

"Then – why not? You have my permission. It is nothing I have not seen coming."

He nodded. "I know. I have known about this night longer than most the other participants, I am sure. Mother told us all about it. I just – If I *am* your future husband, I want our first kiss to mean something beyond a night of ritual and tradition, see?"

My eyes fluttered. "You are the only one to do this tonight so far. You will probably be the only one all night."

He smiled. "And *that* is why I am worthy of you and the Crown. There is more to being King than being King."

"Time's up!" Ella shouted.

Chapter 6

It was my turn to be baffled when Linc stood, kissed my hand, hopped the wall, and left. Not long after, Peter came bursting through the archway. I stood up and rushed to his arms. "Oh, Peter. I can't wait for tonight to be over."

Peter tilted my chin so he could look at my face. "There's dried blood on your lip. Did Linc *bite* you?"

I touched my lip. Sure enough, a little ways inside of my lip was split and there was a spot of dried blood on my lip. I scratched it off. "No. Leo is just an animal, I guess."

"*He* bit you? I'm going to kill him."

"No. It's my own fault. Brian and Christopher ended up being so different than I thought. I gave Leo the benefit of the doubt and let down my guard."

"Anyone hurting you is not your fault. You need to tell your father."

"Of course I'm going to tell Father. That's the whole point of the evening. I report to him about my interactions with each participant and give him my thoughts on them. Leo is not going to be getting a shining review. He's a monster and I'd sooner die than marry him or see him wear the Crown."

Peter quirked a brow. "That's – a rather intense opinion."

I sighed. "Let's not talk about him anymore. Thank you for being concerned for me, though."

"At least I won't have to worry about Stephan or Theo."

"Well, Stephan, at least."

"What happened with Theo on the dance floor? You looked happy."

"Yeah. Dancing with him is always fun. It's just – he was very – flirtatious. It was weird. I am not entirely sure what to expect from him tonight." I yawned.

"You are so cute when you're tired."

"Ella said I was cute when I'm nervous earlier. I hate that I am cute when I want to look angry or fearsome."

"You're cute when you're frustrated, too."

"Shut up, Peter."

"Alright." In one swift move, he pressed his lips against mine. I sighed in relief at the familiar sensation of being in his arms and knowing his heart was mine – at least for the moment. He parted his lips when my mouth opened for a sigh and breathed it in. It was like he was taking away all the negative energy I had stored up from the long evening. Our mouths moved together in a rhythm we knew well. While he had never said in so many words, I knew he loved me. He was only mine as I was only his.

"Time's up!" Ella shouted.

Hesitantly, he pulled away. "Everything will be alright, Rose. Even if your father doesn't choose me in the end, or even if I don't make it, he will be sure an honorable man has your hand. That is the only thing that makes this alright for me."

"I will only be alright if it is your ring on my finger in four months."

"I said, 'Time's up!'" yelled Ella with annoyance thick in her voice.

Peter chuckled. "Better go. I will see you in a couple days, Rose." He kissed me briefly one more time and left.

That's right. They're all going home tonight for their personal final preparations. Thank God I won't have to see them again for a month. And thank God I'll have Peter and Stephan here in a couple days.

I wasn't sure what "final preparations" meant for the noblemen, but apparently, they did. Father had given them instructions on what they needed to do to prepare for next month. He knew I wanted Peter and Stephan with me for the whole month before the King's Test began and he begrudgingly let them prepare a month early.

When he indicated they had an unfair advantage by having an extra month with me, I simply reminded him they already had an unfair advantage because of our friendships. I loved it when I was able to sway Father's opinion during a disagreement; it didn't happen very often.

Stephan arrived just as quickly as Peter did. He looked nervous, which I thought was strange. We had known each other for so long, there was no reason for him to be nervous. He cleared his throat. "Um. Hey. Rose." He stammered out.

I had already taken my seat on the sofa swing again and was gently swinging it. "Hello, Stephan."

He put a finger in his collar and pulled on it like it was choking him. "Just undo the top button," I suggested. "There's no need to feel uncomfortable."

He chuckled dryly as if to say *"Too late,"* but undid it anyway. I patted the empty space next to me and he came over and sat down. Rather than take my hand like I expected, he folded his hands in front of him and looked down.

"Are you alright?" I asked him.

"Uh. Yes. Fine."

"You know, earlier you said a woman is never fine if she says she's fine. I can say the same for you."

"Huh. Touché."

"So…"

"So what?"

"Stephan!"

"Alright, alright, alright. I'm nervous."

"Why are you nervous? It's just me. We've known each other forever."

"*That's* why I'm nervous." He turned to face me and took my hands. "I'm not really sure how to do this, Rose. We've been friends for so long. You've been like a sister to me and now – now I have to try to woo you."

"Woo me?"

He smirked. "For lack of another phrase."

"Well, I would think that should make you feel confident."

He quirked a brow. "Why?"

"Because you know me. You know my likes and dislikes. You know the way I want to rule; we've had that discussion plenty of times. You know the types of things I'm looking for in a husband."

"I do?"

I stopped swinging and turned to face him. "It's not something we've talked about, but I'm sure you can easily figure it out based on how well you know me."

"Hmm." He looked up with his eyes, but not his head, and pursed his lips. "Like you want someone handsome?"

I smiled. "It's not *necessary*, but that's not a concern anyway. All of my suitors are handsome. Think deeper."

He scooted a little closer. That's when it hit me. My *best friend* was going to kiss me. Tonight. What would I think of that?

"Clearly, you need someone intelligent. Someone who can keep up with you in discussion." I nodded. "Someone who can make you laugh when you're sad. Calm you when your short temper flares. Reason with you when you are being unreasonable, but not offend you in the process."

I tried to be offended, but knew my short temper and stubbornness were shortfalls of mine. My smile was still on.

"You need someone who knows your deepest desires and longs to fulfill them. Who looks at you like you are not just the Princess of Arboria, but the Queen of his heart." With each reason, his voice was quieter and he brought his face closer to mine.

"You need someone gentle." He placed his palm on my cheek. "But passionate." He wrapped his other arm around my waist and pulled me close. All I could do was nod. My mouth had dried completely out.

"You need someone who is looking at being King as secondary to being your husband; a man who will love you more than anything or anyone." The hand on my cheek traced down to my upper back. He was good. I had no idea where it had come from. To my knowledge, he had never had a girlfriend.

He moved his gaze from mine down to my lips, then back to my eyes. The nervousness had returned in his expression and for a moment, I thought he wasn't going to kiss me. I exhaled, not realizing I had been holding my breath and that's when he took the opportunity to close the gap and kiss me.

45

He was inexperienced, but there was so much meaning behind his kiss, it didn't even matter. I brought my hands up behind him and pulled myself closer to him. I didn't know what had come over me. I was in love with Peter, right? There was nothing romantic between Stephan and me. Right?

When I ran my fingers through his hair, he groaned and parted his lips. His kiss became demanding and passionate and it was like we couldn't get close enough to each other. I thought I heard someone shouting, but it was muffled against my rapid heartbeat thumping in my ears.

However, he must have heard it because he pulled away, breathing fast. At some point, I had closed my eyes and they stayed closed even when the kiss was over.

"I said, 'Time's up!' Really, Rose. Peter and Stephan have enough of an unfair advantage as it is!" Ella yelled.

Stephan whispered against my still open mouth, "Am I right?"

My eyes fluttered open and I saw he was smiling in a way I had never seen on him before. "Yes," I breathed.

"ROSE!" Ella shouted louder than her previous two commands.

Stephan released me and my limp body fell back against the arm of the sofa. "I'm coming, Ella! Got a little turned around in the maze!" he yelled. "See you in a couple days," he said quietly to me as he got up and left.

"Yeah, right!" Ella shouted at him in response.

What was that*?!*

Chapter 7

Because Theo took the longest of all the men to arrive, I had plenty of time to consider what in God's green earth had just happened with Stephan.

Being four years older than me, Stephan remembered meeting me; I had been two and he was six. According to him, we were immediately inseparable. He didn't have any younger siblings, though he had always wanted one, so he was enthralled with me. He played with me and held my hand if we had to go anywhere. When their visits would end and he had to go home, I cried – so he said.

That was what was so confusing. He had *always* treated me as a younger sister and I had always loved him as an older brother. The thought of him kissing me had actually disgusted me earlier because of those feelings. But then, after the kiss, I had no idea know what to feel. It was like I unexpectedly felt for him what I felt for Peter and that petrified me.

When Theo arrived, I was still limply laying on the sofa.

Theo laughed. "I know it took me a while, but did you really get *that* bored?"

I shook myself out of my thoughts and smiled at him. "Just tired. It has been a long day."

"Come here, Miriam," Theo requested with a curling index finger.

Though I was tired, and more than a little miffed at the gesture, I did as he asked because I knew I would be able to go to bed when his time was up. He took one of my hands and placed it on his shoulder, wrapped one arm around my waist, took my other hand in his and held it to his chest. "Let us dance," he said softly.

I smiled as he pulled me flush against him. "There is no music, Theo."

"We do not need music," he said as he began to slowly sway in a rhythm he set. "Roots, Miriam. You are so beautiful. I have always thought so, but – there is something special about you tonight."

I felt my face turn red and moved my gaze from his eyes to his chest. "Thank you." I turned my head and lay my cheek against him. I was so tired. His heartbeat was steady; he didn't seem to be nervous at all. I sighed in relief. As far as I was concerned, it was a sure sign he wouldn't be up to anything like Leo had been.

"I am sorry it has taken so long for me to get you alone," Theo murmured.

I tried not to frown as I looked back up at him. "What do you mean?"

He stopped moving and released my hand to entwine his fingers together at my lower back. He smirked. "You know."

I narrowed my eyes not unkindly. "Pretend I do not know. Enlighten me."

He began swaying again; only now, he was backing me up toward the sofa swing. "I have held you in my arms so many times on the dance floor – more times than I can count – but the opportunity to do so beyond the dance floor has never presented itself."

"I did not realize you were interested in me beyond the dance floor."

"Who would not be? Look at you. Aside from your incredible beauty, you are graceful and famously kind."

I put my cheek back against his chest. "Please, Theo. You flatter me." The back of my knees hit the swing and buckled underneath me. "Graceful, huh?"

He laughed as I sat down and he lowered himself next to me, not releasing me from his hold. "I am only stating the truth. I will always be honest with you, Miriam."

Then he kissed me. I was grateful it was the end of obligatory kisses for the King's Test. Outside of the evening, I would never *have* to kiss any of them again. And I had every intention of using my kisses judiciously in the future.

He moved his lips against mine, then moved to trace my jawline with them. One of his hands moved to my upper back and he groaned as he pulled me closer and began to kiss my throat. I was stunned still that he would do this, but it felt like his time would be up at any moment, so I didn't stop him, not even when I felt his tongue slide up the side of my neck and his teeth nibble at my ear.

However, when his hand gripped the zipper on the back of my dress and began to pull it down, I said, "Theo, no."

He ignored me and kissed my collarbone as he continued to pull at my zipper. More insistently, I said, "Theo, stop" and twisted my arm behind myself and placed my hand over his to stop the motion.

He stopped, but whispered in my ear, "Come on, Miriam. I know you want it."

I furrowed my brow. "What is it, exactly, that I want?"

"You know," he continued to whisper. "What do you say I meet you up in your suite when my time is up and I will show you how I could please you as your King?" He nipped my ear again.

"I think maybe your time is up, Theo," I said when he started kissing my neck again, but he just nestled himself in closer and I felt his smile on my neck.

"Patience. I promise I will be there tonight."

Seriously? Do I have to spell it out?

"No. You will not."

That did it. He stopped what he was doing and looked at me confused. "There is no need to be shy with me, Miriam. I know you are probably a virgin. I will be gentle with you." My eyes widened. I jumped off the sofa and strode out without looking back.

I passed Ella as she was making her way down the glass hallway. "Rose, what are you doing out here? I haven't said anything about your time being up yet. You're supposed to spend the same amount of time with each man. You still have another minute."

I pointed back to the garden. "I am *not* going back in there with that – that – that – pervert!"

Then, *her* eyes widened. "Pervert? Count Theodore?!"

"YES!" I shouted at her. "Father will understand if I don't spend his one last minute with him."

"No. I'm sorry, but you *have* to go back in there. I'll stand right here and call when the minute is up. Just yell when you make it back there."

"But, Ella!"

"No! I wish I could allow it, but it is my job to make sure the King's Test is executed correctly. Now go. If he tries anything, slap him. You are telling me everything tomorrow."

50

"You will hear about it when Father does," I mumbled as I went back to the center of the maze. When I got there, Theo was laying on his side with one knee up and his other leg dangling of the side of the sofa. He patted the sofa next to him, indicating he wanted me to lay alongside him.

He knew I would have to return! Well, I don't *have to lay next to him.*

"I'm here, Ella! You better be counting the rotting seconds!" I shouted.

"I am!" She responded.

Theo frowned and patted the sofa again. "I'm alright standing," I said as I crossed my arms over my chest, only then noticing my zipper was still undone in the back.

Theo stood and walked over to me. Pointing down, he spun his hand in little circles.

"You will *not* be undoing my zipper tonight or any night if I have anything to say about it, Count Theodore."

"Oooo. Full name. I am in trouble," he teased. "Just turn around. I will zip you back up."

I gave him a dirty look.

"Really, Miriam. I promise. Remember? I told you I would always be honest with you. I may have displeased Your Highness, but I have not lied to you."

Pressing my lips together, I considered the veracity of his claim, then dropped my hands and turned around. "Look, I am sorry, alright? I misread the situation," he said as he zipped me up and I spun back around to face him.

"You 'misread the situation?' The fact that you think I would give myself to you in such a manner tells me you did not only

51

'misread the situation,' but you judged my character completely wrong! What kind of trollop do you think I am?!"

He snickered. "Trollop?"

"Yes. Trollop. Floozy. Butterfly."

"Hey. I never called you a butterfly. I am certain you are not going around flower to flower."

"Roots straight, I'm not! And you will have none of this," I presented myself head to toe with a hand, "unless you win the King's Test." I stepped closer so I was inches from his face and whispered, "And if I have anything to say about it, you will not."

"Time's up!" shouted Ella, as if on cue.

I turned on my heel and marched out of the garden straight up to my room. My assistant, Marie waited for me and helped me out of my impossible gown. I told her I didn't need a bath because I had to wash seven men off my body in a fire hot shower. She laughed and wished me good night as she left.

After showering with the hottest water possible, I crawled into bed and thought about the evening. Brian, Christopher, and Linc had pleasantly surprised me, but Leo and Theo turned out to surprise me negatively. Peter was wonderful, as I thought he would be, but Stephan was, too.

What is going on with Stephan? Could it be that he's in love with me or is he just playing the King's Test? No. He wouldn't play me like that. I'm not really sure what to do with him.

I fell asleep thinking about the seven very different possibilities I was presented that evening.

Chapter 8

The next morning, Father, Ella, and I sat in his office around his small coffee table, sipping our coffee, to discuss the previous evening's activities.

"So, Rose. How would you like to go about this conversation? Shall we discuss by event or person?"

I sighed and rubbed at my temples. "I need another cup of coffee." Immediately after I said it, I heard the scuttling of maid's feet leaving the room to get me another one.

"Was it *that* bad? Really?" Father asked unbelievingly.

Ella snorted. I had already gone through the highlights with her earlier in the morning at breakfast. Father and I both glanced over to her and she gestured with her hand for me to go ahead.

"I think it will be easier to just talk about each person, Father." The maid hustled in and replaced my empty coffee cup with a full one.

"Very well. Though I would like to begin by asking you if anyone stuck out to you, negatively or positively?"

"While I understand, I think that would be best to discuss that as we go, also."

"Of course." He glanced down at his Note-Taker, tapped it a few times and said, "Let's begin with Count Brian of Birch. He has advanced quickly through the ranks of the Royal Arborian Guard. From the outskirts of the dance floor, it seemed like he did not make an excellent first impression."

"No, he did not." I chugged half my second cup of coffee. "During the dance, he boasted about his military prowess and success and it seemed as though he was really only interested in that part of being King."

"What did you say to make him leave confused."

Ella laughed again.

"I told him that there is more to being King than being King."

"Ouch. Was the interview and first kiss any better?"

"You say that like those two things always go hand in hand."

"For the King's Test, they do."

"Touché!" piped in Ella.

Father glanced at her sidelong and said, "Indeed."

I sighed. "The interview went better. He found the center of the maze by climbing the wall and jumping them. He apologized for his idiocy and said he was nervous about interacting with me because he thinks I will be a great Queen someday. I forgave him and he kissed me."

"And…"

"And what?"

"What did the kiss tell you?"

I blanched. "Pardon me?"

"The whole point of the first kiss is that it makes both of you a little vulnerable. He learns something about you and you learn something about him. So. What did you learn about Count Brian?"

"The kiss was about what I had anticipated; it was hard and commanding." Father stiffened. "You asked..."

"So I did. Continue." He unsuccessfully tried to relax by clearing his throat.

"Anyhow, what surprised me was that he was crying tears of humility when it was over. It was real, too. I'm sure of it."

"Crying? Count Brian of Birch was *crying*?" Father asked.

"Yes. It was very strange and actually humbling for me, too. It made me realize that people aren't always precisely what you think."

"Hmm." *tap. tap. tap.* "How about Count Christopher of Alder?"

"I don't think it's any secret how the dance went. He was arrogant and cocky and acted exactly how Arborian's Most Desired is expected to act."

"Why did *he* leave the floor confused?"

"Oh. He had used a line on me and I asked him if it ever actually worked."

"You didn't."

"I did."

"Were you hostile to everyone?"

"No. Only to the ones who deserved it."

"They really *did* deserve it, Uncle," Ella added.

"Thank you, Ella," I said to her.

Father let out an exasperated sigh. "Very well. What of the interview and kiss?"

"He found his way the normal way: through the maze. But when he entered the room, he called out to me like it was hide and seek."

Father pointed his Note-Taker Pen at me. "It kind of was."

I shrugged. "True enough. Then he insulted me and insinuated that it was my idea to kiss all of them and I enjoyed playing head games with people."

"No, he didn't."

"Yes, he did. Father, you're beginning to sound like a twenty-first century teenage girl."

"I have no idea what you mean by that."

"Never mind. I defended myself and he apologized. Then I apologized for my assumptions and we agreed to start over. All he did for his kiss was gently brush his lips against mine."

"Really? Hmm. That says something."

"I thought so, too. I think he really wants to prove himself. After that, I began to doubt all my first impressions and decided to give Count Leonard the benefit of the doubt."

Ella growled quietly. She had demanded immediate castration when I told her about what happened. Her demands for Theo were worse than that.

"How did things with Count Leonard go? You've known each other for some time. Childhood friends."

I scoffed. "Leo is no friend of mine, Father. Hasn't been and I don't think he will be."

He frowned. "I take it things didn't go well."

"No, they didn't. On the dance floor, he almost grabbed my butt and tried to flirt with me. It was uncomfortable. And before you even ask, the reason he looked dumbfounded when he left me on the dance floor was because I turned his logic back in his face."

"What do you mean?"

"He said it was destiny for me to choose him because his mother didn't get chosen during your Queen's Test."

"Ugh."

"That's how I felt, too. I told him that I could use the same logic for his brother."

Father laughed at that.

"As for the interview, I was tired and I was tense and he saw it. Like I said before, at this point, I had been doubting all my first impressions and decided to give him the benefit of the doubt. He noted how tense I was and offered a back massage; something he's famous for in the Court." Father quirked a brow at me. "Hindsight is 20/20, Father."

"What?"

"Never mind. Needless to say, he spoke sweet nothings and his hands roamed all over my back and around my waist, then he kissed my neck. When I turned around in shock, he kissed me passionately, like he had been practicing and imagining it for a long time. I was too shocked to say anything snarky when his time was up and he left."

"So that's a negative for Count Leonard?"

"Yes."

"What about his brother? He always seemed a bit pompous to me."

"Me, too. In fact, that was my first impression tonight on the dance floor, as well. He was boastful, like Brian, but declared himself worthy in *every* area. Apparently, he has been training with Brian on military skills and strategies and he has been observing his father on the demands of a Noble for years. I gave him the same line I gave Brian."

"Mm hmm."

"Like Brian, he began to apologize for his stupidity, but I was done with apologies at that point. He was under extreme scrutiny because of how Leo had behaved. He confessed a childhood crush on me and vowed to prove himself worthy and capable in *all* aspects of being my King."

"And the kiss?"

"No kiss. He said that if he is ever to kiss me, it will mean something beyond tradition."

"Good man."

"So it seems."

"I trust things went well with Peter. You *are* friends with him, right?"

"Of course, I am. Yes. Things went well. Both conversations with Peter were pretty much centralized on how he wanted to rip apart anyone who had offended or molested me. He is very protective."

"Not surprising. The kiss?"

I thought about how to put it. It wasn't *really* our first kiss by a long shot. "It felt – sincere; right."

He looked up from his Note-Taker with his eyes. "Nothing else?"

I shrugged. "He wasn't any more revealing last night than he normally is."

"Alright. And Stephan."

I took a deep breath. "I need another cup of coffee." The maid left again. "Things were definitely different with Stephan. He was similar to Peter on the dance floor, but the interview was very – surprising."

"How so?"

"It began with him making sure I was alright from the rest of the evening, then he said he was nervous because he has known me for so long and the King's Test really changes everything for us. I told him to think of it as an advantage because he knows what I'm looking for. Then he described my perfect man and his kiss – his kiss was so – I can't even describe it. It was odd and wonderful all wrapped up in one. I had been dreading it all evening, thinking it would be like kissing my brother, but it wasn't."

"It wasn't?"

"No."

"Hmm. Count Theodore?"

"Biggest surprise of the evening."

"More than Stephan?"

"By far. I actually walked out on him before his time was up. Ella had to send me back in."

"Interesting…"

"The dance was normal for us. He was a bit more suggestive than normal, but I figured that was just because things were changing. Then, in the interview, he didn't say much that was substantial; we danced to no music and he kissed me almost immediately. His hands roamed more than Leo's, he partially unzipped my dress, and his lips did a bit of roaming themselves. I had to tell him 'No' a couple of times before he actually stopped. Then, he said he would meet me in my room and show me how he can please me as my King. He said he would be *extra gentle* since he figured I was a virgin."

Father snapped his Note-Taker Pen in half. "He said what?"

"That's when I left and Ella sent me back in. He zipped me back up, I told him off, and I left when his time was up."

Father pursed his lips together and his assistant handed him a new Note-Taker Pen. He made a couple scribbles, then turned off his Note-Taker and set it down.

"So. Top two?" he asked.

"Peter and Stephan."

"Not surprised. Bottom two?"

"Leo and Theo."

"Again. Not surprised based on your description of the night's events. You have a good head on your shoulder, sweetheart. I want you to know something. I understand you're irritated and angry that your choice has been taken from you as far as who your husband will be."

"You can't take away what was never mine to begin with."

"I know. But that's how it feels for you. I know that because that's how it felt for me."

"But – You *love* Mother, right?"

"Yes. Very much. We fell in love long before the Queen's Test ever began."

My eyes widened. "What? That's not allowed!"

He laughed. "Doesn't matter. It happened. I suspect something similar is going on with you, too, even if you don't admit it. It's alright. My point is this: as my mother took what I said into consideration and made sure the woman selected would be the right choice, I will do the same for you. Now, I will not guarantee it will be Peter or Stephan. That's partially up to them and how they perform. But knowing who it is you trust most helps me in my decision."

I got up and gave him a kiss on the cheek. "Thank you, Father," I said. When I sat back down, a steaming cup of coffee sat where my second empty one had moments before. I gulped it down and I heard the maid behind me sigh.

Chapter 9

After such a long night and morning, I had a migraine the size of Southland. I dragged myself up to my room and dug around in my bathroom drawers to find something for it. I found the bottle that should have contained the medication, but it was empty.

Lovely. Now I have to go all the way back downstairs to the lab to visit Doctor Winston.

Once I made it outside, I didn't have far to go because Doctor Darrel Winston's lab was right on palace grounds. He was a child prodigy when he was younger and he was only slightly older than me now at twenty-six. He was tallish with a long blond ponytail and wore thick-framed glasses when he was reading or looking at his microscreen. Though he didn't come from a Noble house, I was familiar with him because he had been the Director of the Arborian Science Association for the last five years. When he became Director, he got to move into the Evergreen Palace Science Lab and we had crossed paths at societal functions in the ballroom.

When I entered his lab, he was nowhere to be found in the main area. His examination table lay empty and everything was pristinely clean. Apparently, no one had been sick enough to visit him and he was between experiments at the moment. At least, that was my assumption. I casually walked through the lab to Doctor Winston's open office door.

"Yes, yes. Things are on track," I heard him saying as I walked in. He was at his holostation in the corner in the middle of a comm session.

"Are you certain? Everything has to be perfect," his Britainnian contact was saying.

Doctor Winston must have felt or heard me enter because he turned around and waved me in.

"This is me we're talking about, Quincy. It will all work out as intended. I have to go now, the Princess just came in and I have to see to her," Doctor Winston said.

"Ah. Well. Mustn't keep her waiting. Prince George has been visiting me quite often lately complaining about headaches from the stress his father is putting on him now that he has to find a bride on his own. Your Princess really ran him through with that cancellation," Quincy said. I'm not sure if he was oblivious to the fact that I could see and hear him or if he was just a jerk.

"Not going to discuss politics with you, Quincy. Besides, you know very well how I feel about all that King's Test business. Have a good day," Doctor Winston said.

"Hmph. Night. Goodbye," Quincy mumbled and disconnected.

Doctor Winston stood up out of his seat and gave me a bow. I nodded acceptance and he sat at his desk chair, gesturing for me to sit across from him.

"Sorry to interrupt your call, Doctor," I said.

"Oh. It is alright. Quincy is a bit uptight sometimes," he replied as he waved his hand dismissively.

I laughed. "Well, I would have assured him Prince George would likely have been forced to find his own bride anyway. With how much he has complained about the Council's decision, I cannot imagine him making it very far in the King's Test. Father definitely disapproves of his manners."

Doctor Winston laughed at that. "You are probably right, Princess. What is it that I can do for you on this fine day?"

"As I am sure you know, I had a really long night last night and a long meeting with Father and Countess Elleouise this morning about it. I am having a migraine and am out of my meds for it."

He stood up and walked out to his lab and I followed him. Shifting around bottles in one of his cupboards, he said, "Yes. Those men certainly seemed to be giving you a time last night on the dance floor."

I scoffed. "That was nothing compared to the interviews. I hate this process."

He nodded as if he understood what I was going through, even though he didn't. No one but Father had any clue. Especially not Doctor Darrel Winston. Being both intelligent *and* attractive, he had his pick in ladies.

"Here we are," he said, pulling out a bottle and shaking a few caplets into a smaller container. "I will order you some more, but this should hold you over. You remember how to take them?"

"Yes. Once a day as needed. I thought I was done with these. It has been so long since I have had one."

"Hmm. Did you have one of your dreams last night?" he asked, leaning against the counter with his feet and arms crossed.

Of course. That's *why I have a migraine.*

65

I nodded. "And when was your last migraine?" he asked.

"After my last dream. And you remember what happened there. It scares me, Doctor. How could I have dreamed the results of the vote? There is no way I could have known the Council would vote against foreigners participating in a King's Test. It certainly could have gone either way."

"I have no idea. It is amazing to me how you have these little premonitions. Every time I check your brain, though, everything seems fine. I would not worry too much about it. For now, just accept it and take the caplet when you have a migraine. Would you mind if I took another scan so I can study your brain makeup today?"

"Sure," I said, even though I knew the results would be normal. We made our way down the hall on the left to his scanning room. He directed me to the center of the room where the large, circular scanner descended from the ceiling. As he pressed a myriad of buttons, I heard clicks, beeps, and buzzes as the equipment took its images.

I had been having premonitions for the last couple years and only Doctor Winston knew about it. I hadn't even told Ella. I was pretty sure anyone I told would be convinced I was crazy or needed to be sliced open for experimentation. When he was finished, we walked back to his office and sat again. Looking intently at me, he asked, "Do you want to talk about it?"

I shook my head. "Not really, but this one is probably something you should hear. Maybe. I do not know. It was – different than the others."

"How so?"

"Well, in the past, my dreams have been specific events. Like the Council meeting or my Birthday Ball last year or the boring tea party the Duchess of Birch put on a few months ago. This was vaguer; it was more like a slide show of images."

"What were the images?"

I squirmed a little in my seat. "Seven coffins. Six were made of wood and one of glass. I do not know how, but I know six of the seven participants of the King's Test were in the wooden ones." I paused and bit my lip.

"Who was in the seventh?"

"Me."

His eyes widened. "Oh. Did you see anything else?"

"Count Peter with very blue eyes. Countess Elleouise about twenty years older in twenty-first century clothing. Two children. A boy and a girl. A park bench. Then bright white. After that, I woke up drenched in sweat with a migraine again."

"Interesting."

"The possibilities of the meanings frighten me."

His gaze went past me to the door behind me as he thought. "Well, I have not gotten very far in my psychiatric doctorate yet. Even if I had, there is nothing written about people who have premonitions beyond legends, fairytales, and religion. I will continue looking into it and let you know if I find anything."

"Thank you, Doctor," I said as I stood.

Bowing, he replied, "Anything for you, Princess."

I turned and went back to the palace. Building a mental wall around the dream so I could move on.

Chapter 10

Instead of building the walls I intended on building, I made my way to the library to do my own research on premonitions. The Royal Arborian Library was fascinating to me. So many things were digital nowadays, but we had one of the largest collections of physical books in the world. Because it was one of my favorite places, it didn't take me long to find and pick up a book of fairytales and one on premonitions in religion.

As I sat down at a table, Ella came in, chose a book about Southland and plopped down on a sofa on the other side of the room. First, I scanned through the book of fairytales. Having read it before, it didn't take me long to flip through the whole thing. A common thread throughout it was that the visions were received through magic of one sort or another.

Next, I flipped through the book on religion. Unsurprisingly, the common thread there was that the visions were given through one god or another. I already knew there were stories within my own religion about prophets and such, so I don't know why I expected anything different there.

I walked over to the Computer Desk and did a quick search for scientific reasons for premonitions. There were a lot of theories and hypotheses, but nothing solid. Doctor Winston had claimed there was so scientific data on the subject and this only confirmed his claim.

Sighing, I said, "Come on, Ella. Let's go."

She jumped up, excited. "I'm glad you're *finally* ready to leave!" I shook my head as we left, she had only been there for around a half hour.

The rest of the day passed by rather uneventfully. Father and Mother were meeting with the Petrichoria Delegate and I wasn't expecting Peter and Stephan until the next day. Ella and I spent the afternoon walking through the forest and basking in the sunlight in a patch of wildflowers we found. Though we had hiked through the forest behind the palace many times, it was so large, we were always finding a new spot to explore.

Ella and I decided to spend the evening separate. She hadn't spoken to her family the whole day and I was still pretty tired from the King's Test Ball. Just as I settled into my sofa with a book called *The Hobbit* from the twentieth century, someone knocked at my door.

Sighing, I set my book down and called out for whoever it was to enter. It was the palace Steward. "How can I help you, Steward?"

"Prince George XV of Britainnia is on the holocomm and the King says you need to speak with him because he is busy."

I frowned. "What does he want me to do about it? He is probably complaining again about the Council's decision to not go forward with the Foreigners King's Test."

The Steward smiled. "The King says it is time for you to handle some of the foreign communications since you will be Crown Princess soon."

70

I crushed my eyes closed to defeat the impending headache. "Very well. Patch him through."

As the Steward left, I walked over to my holostation and waited. I let it beep a few times before answering. Prince George's face appeared. As I had figured, he looked frustrated, though more put together than he had been the last time he spoke with Father.

"How can I help you, Prince George?"

He looked taken aback and frowned. "I asked to speak with King Aaron. It is a very serious matter," he said angrily in his thick Britainnian accent.

"I understand that. The King asked that I take the call. He has been in a meeting with our Province Delegate all afternoon and it looks as though it is continuing into the evening. How can I help you?"

He sighed. "I do not think you can. You are only the Princess."

As stars spun in front of my eyes from my anger, I carefully crafted my next response so I didn't create a problem between our kingdoms. "If it is not something I can do on my own, chances are, neither could the King."

"He could not add me to the participant number for the King's Test?"

And there it is. Seriously. This guy needs to take a hint.

"I am afraid not, Prince George. The Council already voted 'nay' on foreigners participating in King's Test for this generation and it is not a decision he can make unilaterally. Surely, he has explained this all before?"

"Yes, he has," Prince George said tightly. "I am sure your Council and King would not want to cause an international incident with this."

I leaned forward. "With all due respect, Prince George, there were ten foreign princes told they were under *consideration* to participate and only four of you have had a problem with the outcome of the vote. The dirty looks you are giving me, and the fact I have never spoken to you before now, tell me that the loss of your chances with me is not the issue. Might I ask why it is so important to you?"

He pressed his lips together. "It is for your kingdom's own good. It has been too long since you have had new blood in your Royal and Noble lines."

I leaned back. "So, you are concerned for our health and well-being? I assure you that while *I* have to marry someone of Noble blood, the regular Nobility marries whoever they want – and they marry outside the Nobility on a regular basis. Furthermore, while I appreciate your concern, it really is not any of your business."

"What was your thought on the process?"

"Pardon?"

"How did *you* feel about foreigners participating in your King's Test?"

"It does not matter how I feel about *any* part of the King's Test, Prince George. I have essentially no say in the process at all."

"I did not ask if you had a say, I asked what you thought." He smirked at me, as if he was getting somewhere now.

I sighed. "To be honest, Prince George, the thought of marrying someone outside Arboria's Nobility did not bother me at all. I think

72

the major obstacle the idea had was that when I was born, the decision of who would participate in the King's Test was already decided.

"It is a long-held tradition with my people, so the men who are participating have been raised knowing they would. When the idea for foreign participation was presented, there was an uproar. Both the Nobles and Delegates from the provinces who will be represented in the King's Test would hear nothing of it. There are twenty votes total and that is twelve votes right there. A few more than that twelve voted 'nay.' As you can see, our hands are tied."

There was a pregnant pause in our conversation as we stared each other down. "I trust that I have assuaged any concerns you have and we will not need to discuss this again. Even if the King *could* have added you in, which I assure you, he cannot, it would be too late. Just last night we had the King's Test Ball, where the seven participants were introduced to the kingdom and me."

He nodded. "Very well. I am not happy, nor will my father be, but I wish you luck. May the right man be selected to lead the beautiful kingdom of Arboria."

"Thank you. Good evening."

He disconnected the call and I went back over to my seat on the sofa, feeling pretty good about the way I had handled things. Another round of knocking came to my door and I discovered it was the Steward again.

"What is it?" I asked when he came in.

"King Michael of Southland on the holocomm. Well-wishing, it seems."

"Father is still unavailable?"

"No. This call is for you. You will probably get a few of these calls throughout the evening tonight."

"Put him through." I picked up my book and walked over to my holostation, readying myself for a long night of talking to well-wishers and whiners.

~ ~ ~

Just as I was getting comfortable in bed, the holocomm beeped again. I considered ignoring it – I had been on the darn thing all evening – but decided I should probably talk to whatever Royalty was comming. I shuffled my way over to the holostation, sat down, and answered while I was yawning.

"Aw. Did I wake you up?" It was Stephan.

"Uh. No. Just heading to bed."

This is already awkward after last night. He had to catch me totally unaware.

"Oh. Good. Uh. Listen. Father and Mother want me to spend a little more time at home, so I'm going to be a week late."

"Oh. That's too bad. Why?"

Don't sound so eager.

He grinned. "Like the rest of Arboria, I'm their favorite to win the King's Test."

I chuckled. "I see. Well, I guess that's understandable. I'll see you in a few days, Stephan."

"In a few, dear Rose," he said and disconnected before I could even think a response.

74

"Dear Rose?"

Part II

Chapter 11

The bright midafternoon summer sun lit my book as I spent the next day in our library. Mother was often telling me to go outside to the field behind the palace, which I had done the whole previous afternoon, but I preferred to spend my time indoors.

Besides, as I always argued, being inside was practically being outside. It was brilliant how our ancestors managed to figure out a way to build everything around the trees. Personally, I didn't know what the engineering behind it was, but when they had to rebuild everything after the Daze epidemic, they thought of everything.

A simple method of removing and filling of materials in the floors, ceilings, and roofs allowed for the trees to continue to grow. Photosynthesis was still possible because of the complicated system of tubes and holes that brought the rain to the roots and sunshine to the leaves. Despite trying to explain it to me in different ways over the years, Doctor Bartholomew, my tutor, had yet to figure a way to make everything stick. Science was simply not my subject.

Knowing life was about to become very busy for me, I took the time to delve into a history book about the twenty-first century. I'm not sure what it was about the time period before the Daze hit, but it intrigued me, enough that I decided to get my Concentration in it when I became a Master in Arborian History.

The book I was flipping through was about the fashions of the era. It was interesting to me how designers would make ridiculous outfits bordering on costumes for their fashion shows, yet the average person wore nothing like it.

As I turned the page and began laughing at a silly outfit the women *actually* wore, I heard the door to the library slide open and an exasperated sigh as the door closed.

"Princess Miriam Petrichoria, I have been looking *everywhere* for you! What are you doing inside on a lovely day like this?" A lock of my long black hair that I could never keep in place, fell out of my braid as I turned suddenly toward the voice.

"Really, Ella? My full name?" I asked.

"Yes. I've been awake for nearly an hour looking everywhere for you. I should have known you would be here reading. What is so interesting *this* time that you would not be enjoying the sun?"

"I *am* enjoying the sun," I defended myself pointing at my book in the sunlight. "Its light is helping me read."

"You know what I mean, Rose." Officially, I was supposed to be called "Princess Miriam," "Your Highness," or "Miss," but my close friends and family always called me "Rose." Ever since I was a child, I have had a borderline obsession with the flower. They were all over my room. I had written a waltz and designed a dance for them. The people had even been calling me the Rose of Petrichoria since I was a child. I wasn't a big fan of the title, but my people liked it, so I let it stand.

"Yes, yes. We can go outdoors in a bit. You have to see this picture I found of twenty-first century fashion!" I waved off her chastisement for staying indoors, looked back to the book, and held it up for her to view the ridiculous fashion. "See!" I showed her the picture of a woman in pink leopard print tight cotton pants with a short pink dress and white flats.

Ella laughed and her short blonde curls bounced. "That's atrocious! Honestly, though, Rose, get out of the twenty-first century and rejoin us here in the twenty-third!"

"Alright, alright, alright," I conceded and stood. On the way out, I set the book on the table next to the door, promising myself I would come back later and put it away.

Arm-in-arm, Ella and I made our way down the long hall to the Core, guards trailing behind us for protection. The room was thus named because it was the center of and entrance to Evergreen Palace. From it, hallways and stairways branched out to different rooms and areas. I would imagine coming to Evergreen Palace without knowing how to get around would be rather daunting, but, being raised here, I knew every little nook and cranny.

Trying to sound nonchalant as we exited the Core to make our way to the field behind Evergreen Palace, I asked, "Has Count Peter arrived yet?"

Ella gave me a quirked brow and side grin as she said, "No. I heard he won't be arriving until late this evening."

I grunted in disappointment before I could stop myself and Ella laughed. "Honestly, Rose. Do you think you can hide your secret romance from me?"

Stopping her on the steps down to the first floor, my eyes widened and I hushed her. "I thought I had! But if you know, keep it down," I whispered with a tinge of fear of being found out.

Ella just laughed more as if I wasn't doing something expressly forbidden by my parents by being in a relationship with Peter. I sighed and pinched the bridge of my nose.

"Rose, don't worry so much! You know I would never tell!" Ella assured me. "Besides, Uncle admitted he and Auntie were in love before their Queen's Test. I'm sure he would understand."

"All the same, please keep it to yourself." I looked back at her with a slight smile. "So is he really arriving late tonight or were you simply yanking my roots?"

"Oh, he really is coming in late. I overheard Aunt Amoura discussing it with the palace Steward."

"Oh." I was disappointed.

How can I greet him if I don't know when he'll arrive? Would it look suspect if I waited up? Yes. Probably.

"I heard Count Stephan will be late as well," I sighed. Ella sighed, too. The four of us had friends for a very long time, even though we ladies rarely got to see the gentlemen and the gentlemen only saw each other when they were with us. "But *he'll* be late by a week."

"A week?!" Ella asked with the question of "why" implied thickly.

"Yes. Apparently, his parents want him to be home for a little while longer before he's gone for this time plus three months of the King's Test – and possibly forever."

"Well, they're rather confident of him."

I shrugged. "They have no reason not to be. He's more qualified than the other participants." I bit the corner of my bottom lip.

"More qualified than Count Peter?" Ella asked, knowingly.

I nodded as I thought about it. Everyone in the kingdom knew that Stephan was the most likely to make it to the end; he was a favorite already.

"Have you and Count Peter talked about what will happen if – you know?"

"No," I responded sadly. "I think we already know what will happen if he doesn't make it to the end."

The King's Test was the traditional method of selecting the next King of Arboria, also commonly referred to as my husband. If I had been a boy, it would have been the Queen's Test to determine the next Queen. Throughout the Test, eligible noblemen take part in the mysterious trials known only to the King and Queen, and in some circumstances the Council, before it begins. As time progresses, men are eliminated from the Test until two are left. At that point, Father will choose the one he deems most fit to be my husband and King. If Peter wasn't in the final two – well, that was not something I wanted to think too long about.

We stayed quiet as we walked in the field of purple and yellow wildflowers. Things had always been that way with Ella, my best girl-friend and cousin. For as long as I could remember, we could just be together without saying anything at all. Because our fathers were brothers, we were practically raised together.

Ella was the Countess for the Maple Province, which was just outside our capital city of Petrichoria. Lucky for us, her family's estate was just on the border, making visits easier. If she ever needed to, she could always send for something to be brought for her and it would arrive within a couple hours.

After a good half hour, Ella and I lowered ourselves to the ground, laying back and watching the light grey clouds roll by. I was glad for her easy company. Father and Mother had been stressing me out over the last week with the preparations for the three big events coming up. On August 31, I would be turning twenty-one, what our culture saw as the age of wisdom and maturation. There would be a magnificent ball with dancing, conversing, sampling foods, and just overall frivolity.

On September 1, my Crowning Coronation ceremony would take place. Being the Princess, I would already inherit the Crown should anything happen to my parents, but this was our kingdom's way of acknowledging the people had faith in my ability to become Queen one day. If we had been dependent on a Regent, it would also be the time he or she would relinquish the Crown.

The following day, September 2, would be the beginning of the King's Test. Because my parents were the only ones who knew anything about it, I honestly had no idea what to expect. I would find out each part as the gentlemen did.

"Ella?" I broke the silence after a good while and apparently woke her up because she snorted herself awake. I laughed and she wrinkled her nose at me. "I'm sorry, Ella," I said through my giggles even though we both knew I really wasn't.

She turned and looked at me with her sparkling blue eyes. "I was having a perfectly good nap, so you better have something good to say, oh glorious Rose of Petrichoria."

It was my turn to wrinkle my nose at her. "Thanks for that, Ella. You're a real gem." She knew my opinion on the title and took every opportunity she could to make fun. As her laughing died down, I asked her what was on my mind. "When do you think your parents will start nagging you about marriage?"

She furrowed her brow and made a grunty sound of disgust. "Blossoms, Rose. I have no idea. They haven't yet, but I'm guessing after you're married in four months, it will soon begin."

I smiled. "I'll do my best to be there for you when it begins. It's horrid. Father and Mother have been talking nonstop lately about the King's Test, which leads to discussions about the Royal Wedding, which lead to discussions about the Crowning Coronation for the future Prince. It's enough to drive me crazy!"

"I can see how that would be annoying and nerve-wracking. I guess I hadn't really thought about anything past the King's Test for you. You know I'll stay here as long as you want me to, right? Even past my duties as Crown Princess' Maiden."

I took the hand of my cousin and gave it a little squeeze. "That's good to know. Thanks, Ella."

Pretty soon, we had fallen silent again. I closed my eyes and listened to the gentle breeze blow over the wildflowers. They smelled so beautiful – not nearly as beautiful as my rose maze – but lovely all the same. Focusing on my breathing, I let the stress I had release from my body to make way for the new stress about to hit hard.

"Princess Miriam! Countess Ella!" We heard our names being yelled. Ella snorted herself awake again and we both giggled.

Both sitting up, we turned around to see the palace Steward looking over the tall field trying to find us. "Over here!" I yelled and waved in a most unladylike fashion.

The Steward shook his head, but said nothing of my lack of manners. "It is time for supper, miladies!" He yelled only because he was so far away from us.

"We will be right in!" I yelled back for the same reason. Ella and I stood up and brushed the grass and dirt from our rears. We had been having a dry spell lately, so it easily slid off our clothing. Unfortunately, I had decided on ivory pants that morning and didn't consider it before lying in the grass.

Marie is not *going to be happy about these stains.*

When we made it to the Dining Hall on the second floor, Father and Mother were already waiting at the ridiculously large dining table. I was never sure why we had one so big; we never had so many guests at Evergreen Palace.

Perhaps for the Crowning Coronation we'll have enough to fill it. No. That's unlikely since tickets are drawn from a lottery. The Royal Wedding?

"Princess Miriam, must you dawdle when you are summoned? Your father and I have been waiting for quite some time! Hello, Countess Elleouise."

I grimaced at the use of my real name and Ella waved politely as we took our seats near my parents.

"Now, Amoura. Rose has been under quite a bit of stress lately. I don't blame her for taking a well-earned rest." Father said as he leaned over and gave Mother a kiss. "Also, there is no reason to be so formal when it's only us."

Mother blushed. She always had been putty in Father's hands and I appreciated him using this to my advantage. The love they had for each other also gave me hope for my own future. Mother, after all, had to participate in the Queen's Test to become Father's bride.

"I suppose you're right, Aaron," she said to him. Looking back to me and taking my hand, she apologized. "I'm sorry, Rose. I suppose I'm a little overwhelmed as well, though I'm sure your stress dwarfs mine. I tend to become a little green-berried when I am."

"A little?" Father joked. Mother lovingly nudged him with her elbow. "How did your conversation with Prince George go last night, Rose?"

Ella shot me a look. I hadn't told her about it. "It was – fine." I had blissfully put the conversation out of my mind and did not really want to go through it. I sighed. "He wanted you to make a special exception and have him included in the King's Test. I told him, congenially, that it wasn't in your power to make a unilateral decision like that and that the participants had already been announced, so it was too late."

"Hmm. What did he say?"

"Well, he wasn't happy. At one point in the conversation, he threatened future conflict over it. By the end, I think he had finally resigned himself to the fact he won't be joining us."

86

"What is *with* that kingdom? Ever since boundaries were redrawn centuries ago, they have been trying to lay claim to different parts of the continent."

"They're probably still bitter over losing it in the first place."

Ella snorted at that.

I smiled at her, then turned by attention back to Father. "I also received several other calls of well-wishing from other world leaders and whining from three other Princes who got excluded from the King's Test. All those conversations went about the same as Prince George's."

"Who else complained?"

"Let's see," I had to think about it because of the numerous calls I had received. "Prince Jean of Swiss-France, Prince Xi Roger of the Chinese Empire, and Prince Harold of Scandinavia."

"I should have never even let them know about the possibility."

I nodded. When he decided to call around to the ten selected kingdoms, I told him that, but he hadn't listened to me.

The rest of dinner was uneventful, but nice. We talked about how the Maple Province was faring, how Ella's little brother, Thomas, was doing with his geography lessons, and how her parents' recent anniversary ball went – we weren't able to attend because we were having another meeting with the Province Delegates about the upcoming King's Test.

As uncomfortable as it was for Ella, it was a relief to have Mother asking about her suitors and her plans for the future rather than focusing on me. Ella was gracious and answered all her questions. When she told Mother she didn't currently have any suitors because of her duties in the upcoming King's Test, Mother tried to pry out information about who she would be interested in when it was all over.

After several times dodging the question, which was asked in numerous different ways, Ella finally relented while we were sipping at some after dinner wine. "Oh. I don't know. I suppose of the seven eligible noblemen, I would have to say Stephan Oak."

"Well," Mother began in a gossipy tone, "You know he's a favorite among the people for the King's Test."

"Amoura…" Father said in a slight warning.

"What? It's not like she doesn't know."

"Oh, yes. I'm well aware that Stephan will probably be one of the final two," Ella interrupted.

Mother turned her attention to me and I flicked Ella hard on her outer thigh for purposefully making that happen. Ella just smiled, proud of herself.

"Rose, dear. If Stephan Oak was one of the final two, would you want him? After all, you *have* been friends for most of your lives."

I twirled the last sip of wine in my glass and stared at it. "I suppose it would depend on how the King's Test goes. Perhaps one of the other gentlemen would be better suited after all."

Mother scoffed. "Like who?"

Pretending to really think hard about it, I stopped twirling my glass and looked to the ceiling. "Well, what about Peter?"

"Peter Juniper? Certainly you can't be serious! I mean, I *know* you have been friends for years, but the young man takes nothing seriously. He would probably be a good husband, but a King –"

"I think Peter is a fine young man," Father intruded with a knowing grin. He always was perceptive. "It takes more than book-smarts to be King, Amoura. You know that."

Mother sighed. "You're right, of course, Aaron." She reached over and held my hand. "Peter Juniper is a good man and knows you well. Let's hope at least one of the two end up in the final two. It would be nice for you to not have to start practically from the seed with someone. Though, I will tell you I prefer Stephan to Peter. He's smarter, more charming, more –"

"We're going to bed now, ladies," Father interrupted again with a smile. Mother frowned. "Goodnight." He and Mother gave us kisses on the cheeks, then made their way out.

It had become late and the wine had prepared us for a good night's sleep. Ella and I went to the stairway in the Core to go to our rooms. While I had to go all the way to the fifth floor, Ella's guest suite was on the third floor, so I walked her there before going the rest of the way up.

Giving me a hug, Ella said, "Good night, Rose. Things will work out. Aunt Amoura will love you no matter who you marry."

"I'm not sure why it matters so much to her what I think. It's not like it's *my* choice anyway." I sighed. "Oh well. Good night."

I gave her a squeeze, then released her to enter her room. As I made my way up two more floors to my room, I thought about how lucky I was with the life I had. My family led a kingdom and the people loved us because we did our best to be good to them. My parents loved me and each other. I had dear friends who knew me well. And Peter. I had Peter; even if it was only for another month.

When I entered my room, my assistant, Marie, was patiently waiting on my chocolate brown sofa reading a magazine about current fashion to keep me on trend. As was our custom, she stood and curtsied gracefully. "Good evening, Princess Miriam. I have prepared your bath just the way you like it."

"Thank you, Marie." The door slid closed behind me and I walked into the bathroom, Marie following a few steps behind. After I had pulled off my grass-stained ivory trousers, which she *did* frown at, and removed my forest green sleeveless top, Marie helped unlace my corset.

Letting out a large breath, I told her, "I was born in the wrong era, Marie. Did you know back in the twenty-first century, women did not need to wear corsets?"

"Technically, we do not *need* to wear them now, either. It has just been in style for decades."

Arching my back after it was removed, I replied, "Well, maybe it is time for the *style* to change. Perhaps I will start a trend by no longer wearing corsets."

Marie quirked an eyebrow at me knowing I wouldn't stop wearing them, but politely didn't say anything past her smug grin. Maybe some other Royals or Nobles would have a problem with their assistants doing such a thing, but Marie had been with me for quite some time and I allowed her certain liberties others didn't have.

"I have laid out your night gown and undergarments on the bed, Your Highness. Have a good night," she said as she turned on her heel and pushed the frame button to slide the door shut.

Dipping a toe in first, I tested the heat of the rose-scented water. Pleased with how wonderfully hot it was, I submerged the rest of my body into the large tub. Allowing the heat to seep into my muscles, I rolled my neck, wrists, and ankles. After simply soaking for a while, I used my rose-scented shampoo, conditioner, and soap.

When I had yawned for the tenth time, I decided it was time to get out and go to bed. I towel-dried with my bath sheet and wrapped it around my body as I left the bathroom and padded over to my bed across the room.

Marie left me a short emerald green night gown with thin sleeves because the summer heat was nearing its peak at around 98°F. I slipped it on, then lay on top of the blankets. Taking a cleansing breath for the night, I reached and swiped my hand over the light panel on the wall next to my bed.

Though my window was dimmed for the night, I could still see the green light of the Space Needle faintly. A reassurance that all was well and I was safe to fall asleep. Knowing I would see Peter in the morning, I closed my eyes and began to drift to sleep.

Chapter 12

Just as I was about to give in to sleep, my brain turned back on and I remembered the book I had promised myself earlier I would put away later. Later had come and gone and I had forgotten. I knew it could wait until morning and that I could even have a housekeeper take care of it, but I was particular about the organization of my twenty-first century history books. Everyone knew it, too, so no one dared touch them.

Sighing, I rolled out of bed and left my room. My Guard was surprised to see me up and out again, but said nothing. It wasn't completely unheard of for me to make my way to the library late at night. He followed me as I made my way to the fifth floor Core, down the stairs, and back to the library.

Grabbing the book without looking or stopping as I entered the library, I hustled to the spiral tree stairs on the right of the room and climbed up to the fourth floor of books. The ladder was where I had left it earlier when I took the book from the shelf, so I knew it would be a quick trip to and from the library.

Tucking the book under my arm and holding it in place with the same hand, I climbed the ladder single-handedly until I could reach the twelfth shelf. As I balanced my feet on the rung I stood on, I let go of the ladder momentarily to take the book from under my arm and put it back where it belonged.

"Oh, Rose," I heard my name drawn out and it startled me. At the same time that I gasped, I lost my balance and windmilled my arms desperately to stay on the ladder, to no avail. I didn't even have time to process that I was falling before I did, and was caught in someone's arms.

I let out an ugly "hoomph" as I landed and panted as my heart raced. The person who caught me was laughing and that was when I realized who it was.

"Count Peter Juniper! You scared me nearly to my death! Put me down!" I slapped his shoulder and he put me down, still laughing and still holding my waist.

"Oh, come now, Rose. What was scarier, my voice or falling off the ladder?" Peter asked as he took my hands and tried to look at my face.

Irritated, I looked up at him and shrugged. "Falling off the ladder."

He moved his hands to my hips and pulled me closer to him. I crossed my arms. Mother was right about one thing: he never took anything seriously; apparently not even falling off a ladder. "And I caught you, right?"

I huffed. "Right."

"So, technically speaking, I saved you more than I scared you." He was smugly grinning at me now with his straight white teeth and disarming smile.

I unfolded my arms and put my hands on his shoulders. "How is it possible that you can so easily talk yourself out of trouble with me?"

Peter brought his lips to mine and kissed me briefly. "I'm devastatingly charming and handsome."

I laughed. "And so humble, too." I leaned my head against his chest and hugged him. Even though we saw each other only a couple nights before, the ball was so formal and it had been very long before that. "I missed you, Peter. How did you find me up here?"

He put his cheek on my head. "I've been hanging out in the library since I got here. I figured you would make your way here sooner or later."

I smiled and pulled back to look at him again. Even though we only got to see each other every couple months, he knew me so well. While I hadn't known Peter as long as I had known Ella or Stephan, he and I had clicked the first time we danced at a ball five years ago. Beyond his aforementioned smile, chocolate brown eyes, and wavy blonde hair, there was something about him that pulled me to him.

His joking smile turned into a genuine small one. Pressing his forehead against mine, he muttered sincerely, "Sweet tree blossoms, Rose. I've missed you, too."

Suddenly remembering that I didn't put on a robe, I jumped, hitting my nose against his chin. We both said, "ow" at the same time. As he removed his hands from me and rubbed at his chin, he asked, "What is it?"

Rubbing my nose, I stuttered, "I – Well, you see –" Then it all came spilling out at full-babble speed. "It was just supposed to be a quick trip to and from the library. I didn't expect to see anyone, much less *you*, so I didn't bother putting on a robe and it's really, really hot, so Marie laid out just a little gown thingy so I wouldn't roast overnight, so now I'm just a little embarrassed at how much of me is showing and – "

Peter put a finger to my mouth to stop my verbal waterfall, grinning the whole time. "I promise not to look at anything but your face for the rest of the evening."

"Thank – hold on. What do you mean 'for the rest of the evening,' Peter?"

He laughed. "I didn't look up when you were on the ladder, if that's what you're worried about. However, how could I resist looking at your long legs and lithe arms?"

"I'm five-four, Peter. How long can my legs really be?"

He shrugged. "They're lovely all the same."

I rolled my eyes, but couldn't help blushing as I pointed at him. "Alright, Peter. I can't fault you for that. But no more. You be a gentleman."

He nodded and joked in a snooty voice. "Yes, of course. I must prepare myself for the King's Test."

Though I had been smiling with him, my smile quickly faded and I looked down. "Why did you have to go and bring *that* up?"

He tilted my chin so I was looking at him. I was very sensitive about the King's Test. I didn't feel it was fair for my choice of a husband to be taken from me. At least I was able to talk the Council out of their idea to have the participants comprised of foreign princes to create an alliance between nations. While I personally didn't mind one way or another, I really had no option either way, I knew there was a faction in Arboria that wasn't fond of the idea. As I said before, Father had been so certain they would be for it, he had already contacted several Kingdoms about the idea; some were not very happy about the cancelation of the plan.

A tear fell from my eye before I could stop it and he wiped it away with his thumb. "I'm sorry, Rose. I didn't mean to spoil our meeting. Please forgive me. I'm sorry."

I sniffled most romantically and we both laughed. Blinking away my tears, I told him it was alright and kissed him. Pulling away, he held my hand and we climbed down the tree stairs of the library.

When we left and walked slowly up the stairs of the Core and back to my room, the Guard once again followed at a respectable distance. I knew he wouldn't say anything to anyone. Marie had told me my night Guard and day Guard were both very trustworthy and loyal gentlemen and that was enough for me.

We said nothing as we crossed the Core and climbed the spiral stairway. The Guard took his post when we made it back to my room and Peter gave me one more kiss before I said good night and entered my room.

Letting the door slide closed behind me without a second glance, I quickly walked over to my four-poster bed and laid down on top of the blankets again. This time I grabbed one of my extra pillows and squeezed it.

Yes. Life is good.

I took a final deep breath and fell asleep for the rest of the night.

Chapter 13

"What kind of fun plans do we have today, Rose? Deciding the color of the flowers for your Birthday Ball?" Peter was joking with me at breakfast with Ella and my family.

Stoically, I responded, "Actually, Peter, that *is* on my to-do list for the day. I am really looking forward to your opinion on such an important matter."

Peter's face blanched and I laughed, which made everyone else laugh as well. "I'm kidding with you, Peter. That is something I am going to do today, but I was planning on bringing Ella with me. We will also be looking for the wedding in a few months. You are welcome to join us for it, of course. The flower fields are always beautiful this time of year."

Peter put both hands up in surrender. "I think I'm going to pass on that one, but I'd *love* to sit in on your tutoring session. It's so much fun to push Doctor Bartholomew's buttons." Peter's eyes glinted with mischief.

"You're welcome to join me, but it is my final lesson, so we will have to pay *some* attention to him or he'll get cross. Ella, will you be joining us for that?"

Ella shook her head and snorted. "No thank you. I think I will help Aunt Amoura with anything she needs for the upcoming ceremonies instead." In other words, she had no desire to listen to Doctor Bartholomew pontificate on important Arborian traditions or ancient history.

During all of this, my parents were sitting next to each other watching us with giant smiles on their faces. I think it made them glad to see me happy rather than stressed out of my mind.

Looking up when I heard the door to the Dining Hall slide open, I saw the palace Steward come in. Though I expected him to walk to over to Father, he came to me instead.

"Your Highness, Count Stephan Oak has holocommed for you and is waiting for you to answer."

"Excellent. Please put the comm through to my office." I ignored the googly eyes Ella made and the curious glances from everyone else at the table. Placing my napkin down and standing up, I excused myself from the table and walked to my office. I sat down at my holostation and answered. Stephan's image popped up in front of me; he ran his hand through his light brown hair when I answered and gave me a smile that stretched all the way to his eyes.

"Hello, Stephan."

"Princess Miriam, so nice to speak with you," he said in an oddly formal voice.

"So nice to speak with you, as well, Count Stephan," I said, mimicking his tone and formality.

He looked down and laughed realizing how ridiculous he sounded. He pinched the bridge of his nose. "Sorry, Rose. You wouldn't believe the pressure being put on me here at home about the King's Test."

"Of course not. I have no stress here at all," I said sarcastically and crossed my arms playfully.

He laughed again and folded his arms on the desk in front of him. More serious, he said, "I'm sure you've heard the people talking. To be honest with you, it is making me feel a little uncomfortable with you. Almost like I'm not sure how to be with you anymore. I mean, the other night – " I grimaced, expecting an apology. "No. I'm not apologizing for it. It was just so –"

He can always read me so well.

I smiled. Stephan's honesty was always something I appreciated. "– different," I finished for him. "Yes, I've been hearing the latest gossip." There had been dozens of broadcasts from different stations on the holocomm discussing the nature of Stephan and my relationship. Arboria was definitely in love with the idea of us being in love.

I folded my arms on my desk and leaned forward a little. "But nothing needs to change between us, Stephan. It's not like we're at the end of the King's Test right now."

"No, but the closer it gets, the more nervous I become."

Maybe I misread him the other night.

I looked down at my hands. There was an awkward silence. I broke it. "You know, Stephan. If you don't want to participate in the King's Test, it's alright. I will not be offended. I'll understand, in fact. I know we have always had a sibling-type relationship with each other and the change in our status is – interesting." I shrugged. "You have every right to be able to choose the woman you marry."

Stephan sighed. "That's why I'm so nervous, Rose. Out of all the women I know, you are by far the most intelligent, kind, loving

– beautiful one. I'm not sure there *is* anyone else I would want to marry." I looked up at him.

"Oh." It was all I could say through my shock. This was certainly not the conversation I thought we would be having. Stephan and I had been best friends for as long as I could remember, but I never knew he felt this way. I looked at my hands in front of me again. I vocalized the thought. "I had no idea you felt that way."

"I wasn't going to tell you. I haven't told you already because I didn't think it fair for you to have my feelings on your mind during the Test. I do *not* want you to feel any obligation to me because of who I am and how I feel. I just – I couldn't keep it to myself anymore. Not after the other night. Not when it's quite possible we'll be married in only a few short months."

"No. I mean, yes, it *is* quite possible, but no, I don't feel any obligation. I am glad you told me." I tried to give him a genuine smile, but inside, I was screaming.

I'm already confused from the other night. Now – this? He wants to marry me? Does that mean he loves me? What else could it mean?

If my parents caught wind of this and it somehow ended up being Stephan and Peter in the final two, Father would choose Stephan for sure, regardless of my opinion. The fact that I might not mind perplexed me.

He smiled back and sighed. "Good. Well. I'm glad to get that off my chest. I'm looking forward to seeing you in a few days, Rose."

"You, too, Stephan. Have a good day."

"You, too. Bye." He disconnected.

"Bye," I said after his image had already disappeared.

Chapter 14

I was quiet during Ella's and my trip to the flower fields. Actually, I was pretty quiet the whole visit. Marie was with us and took notes on which flowers we liked and she said she would take care of placing the order when we returned to the palace.

It didn't take Ella and me long to figure out which flowers we would use for my Birthday Ball. Most of them would be roses, as everyone surely expected. When we were finished, we had another quiet ride back to Evergreen Palace. Although it had not taken long to choose the flowers, traffic had been unusually terrible and it caused me to be late for my tutoring session.

With everything else going on, I didn't want to meet with Doctor Bartholomew. I already achieved my Mastery in Arborian History, as was required of all heirs to the Crown. There was really no reason for him to insist on this final meeting before declaring me ready to become Crown Princess, besides his own arrogant stubbornness.

At that moment, I was more concerned about the new developments with Stephan. Why was I not opposed to his affections? I knew I loved Peter, but there was something new stirring inside me for Stephan. Is that why heirs weren't supposed to get into relationships before the King's Test? Because it presented all kinds of confusing situations and emotions?

As Ella walked me up to the tutoring room, she stopped and said, "Alright. Spill it, Rose," exasperatingly when we were about halfway there.

Not realizing I had zoned off or had been as quiet as I was, I shook my head to bring myself back to reality and smiled at her. "It's nothing, Ella. Don't worry."

"It's not nothing. You've been all out of sorts since you got off the comm with Stephan earlier. Is he not coming after all?"

"Oh, no. He's coming."

"Then what?"

We had reached the second floor at this point and I stopped short of leaving the Core steps. Quietly, I told Ella, "He's in love with me."

"What?!" She did not respond quietly and I shushed her. Now at a whisper, she said. "He's decided to tell you this *now*?"

I nodded and continued walking. "Well, he didn't so much *say* he is in love with me. He said he didn't want to marry anyone else and he couldn't keep it to himself anymore with the possibility of marriage looming in the near future. Who knows how long he has felt this way."

"Geez. I can see how that would put you out of it. Are you going to tell Peter?"

I sighed. "I don't know. I haven't decided yet. I probably should."

"I agree. He has to know what he's up against. Before, it was just Stephan, but Stephan in love? He's going to be tough to beat."

"Yeah, especially considering the fact that I'm not sure how I feel about it."

Before she could respond, we arrived at the tutoring room. Peter was waiting outside, leaning on the door with his arms and legs crossed.

Tutting, he said, "Doctor Bartholomew is not going to be happy, Rose. You're late."

I released Ella and gave him a hug. "He will be alright." Pulling away to look at him, I said, "I need to talk to you after we're done here, alright?"

Furrowing his brow, he said, "Alright. Is everything alright?"

"I think so. I just found out some information I think you should be privy to."

He nodded and offered me his arm, which I took. Ella and I waved each other goodbye, as Peter and I made our way into the room.

"Princess Miriam, Count Peter. How lovely for you to finally join me," Doctor Bartholomew said with a twist of insincerity in his voice.

I laughed as Peter and I sat on the sofa opposite his desk. Peter had been right, of course. Doctor Bartholomew was very unhappy. However, when he tried to look angry and intimidating, he never really pulled it off. He ended up looking like an unhappy cat.

"I'm sorry, Doctor Bartholomew. I had an unexpected comm regarding the upcoming King's Test, then flower shopping went long. It won't happen again." I smirked at my joke and Peter pursed his lips to stop himself from laughing.

Doctor Bartholomew wagged his finger at me and smirked in return. "Very funny, Princess." He wasn't *that* much older than me, only ten years, but he sometimes behaved like he was as old as my parents.

Entwining his fingers on his desk, he jumped right into our final lesson. "Do you remember what caused the creation of our kingdom, Princess?"

I rolled my eyes. "Are we really going to discuss this? It's basic history that *anyone* older than ten in the kingdom should already know."

Doctor Bartholomew just stared at me and cleared his throat.

Sighing, I said, "Very well. Arboria was founded as a result of the Oramatosis pandemic." I hated talking about Oramatosis.

"And what was Oramatosis?"

Peter leaned back in his chair and closed his eyes.

I wish I could take a nap right now.

Doctor Bartholomew cleared his throat again.

Leaning back in my own chair, I sighed again and explained, "Oramatosis, more commonly referred to as the Daze, was unintentionally created and released by Doctor Jason Douglas, who synthesized a virus to carry genetic cargo discovered in archived human genome samples that was thought to expand the mind. Douglas thought it would allow the mind to retain more knowledge and see patterns and connections between data already known – so that one could maximize their ability to both ingest and synthesize data. He also thought it would not be communicable. The expansion of the mind was something he desired only for himself.

"Unfortunately, the genetic cargo carried by the virus was damaged in the process. Rather than provide a beneficial alteration to the genetic code, it became a self-replicating prion factory – producing mis-folded proteins that slowly consumed ones faculties whilst destroying their brain matter. It was released through Douglas, and his many interactions with other people, all over the world."

All the scientific words rolled off my tongue like I knew what I meant, but I didn't really, exactly know. All I knew was that the virus did something it wasn't supposed to do and everyone from then on was rooted.

"With an unhealthy dose of arrogance, Doctor Douglas declared himself the savior, championing a foundation, bearing his own name, offering treatments and hope for cure. The cure would never come, at least not from him. It could never come from him. Doctor Douglas knew this, but he enjoyed concocting treatments funded by masses that were also desperate to be his personal test subjects. No one would know until much later that he was the selfish creator of Oramatosis. He was sick. He was a monster. Everyone knows the name Douglas. The Firs no longer bear his name."

A few years ago, I had to do a presentation on the Oramatosis pandemic. It was supposed to be a manuscript speech, so I rehearsed it at least a thousand times. It was still memorized.

I continued. "The problem was that the Daze killed the portion of the brain that paralyzed a person as he slept. It killed the portion that upon awakening allowed him to realize it was all just a dream. It killed the piece that tempered the frightening, evil imagery that is borne out of the depths of fear, resulting in people living in an awakened nightmare.

"The subject would lose all grip on actual reality and only see and experience the nightmare. It wasn't constant; it would happen at random times. Dreamers could be eating a bowl of cereal and be slapped out of reality to find themselves slouched behind a dumpster defending themselves from a starved mountain lion wandering the streets. There was never a warning. They might be pulled back to reality only to discover that they had actually wandered out of their house into the middle of the street, having crushed a helpless bird in their shaken bloodied hands. Shame followed the Dazed, their innocence stolen from them while they lived their fears."

"Hold on. Is this the manuscript speech you wrote?" interrupted Doctor Bartholomew.

"Yes," I answered, then continued without missing a beat.

"Eventually, the subject *would* be in a constant state of living nightmare. If the nightmares didn't eventually drive the subject to some sort of suicide, the subject would eventually die of malnutrition, starvation, dehydration, heart attack, or some traumatic injury from a Dazed episode.

"By the time people realized that no part of the Douglas Foundation was actually working towards curing the disease, it was too late. Seeing people experience the Daze became commonplace and, eventually, the Daze had infected nearly everyone on the planet."

"Very good. Now, tell me about the cure. Where did it come from?"

"A gentleman by the name of Doctor Joshua Davidson had an immunity to the Daze and a vaccine cure, Soteria, was developed from samples of his blood collected at the scene of his murder. Later, it was discovered Jason Douglas hired men to kill him.

"The vaccine cure was the first of its kind. For some time, scientists had been trying to find ways of creating such a thing for a variety of illnesses. Soteria opened the door for scientists to develop more vaccine cures for a variety of deadly diseases.

"My ancestor, Alexander Nicholls, was a reporter who received a tip regarding the creation of the vaccine cure and began investigating it. Every lead he followed led to more evidence and the investigation nearly cost his life at the end of it. By the time he found someone willing to take the risk – of becoming a target for Douglas – to mass produce the cure, some people were so far gone into the Daze, they didn't notice it. Some people knew about it, but were skeptical, so they didn't accept it. Some people that never took the Daze injection didn't see a reason to take it. But there were some who took the injection and became cured or immune to the Daze."

"What happened to the people who never had the Daze, but never accepted the vaccine cure?"

We were suddenly interrupted by Peter snoring loudly. Doctor Bartholomew walked over to him and smacked him upside the head. Peter jolted awake, rubbing the back of his head and glaring at Doctor Bartholomew.

"If you are going to insist on sitting in on Princess Miriam's final class, *I* am going to insist you do not become a distraction."

I covered my mouth to stifle a laugh and Peter smirked at me. I said to Peter, "I told you he would be cross if you did not listen." He hadn't really been sleeping; he was trying to get on Doctor Bartholomew's nerves and succeeded.

"I am sorry, Doctor. I had a late night traveling and must have dozed off."

Doctor Bartholomew gave Peter a dirty look, then repeated his question to me.

"Those who never had the Daze but never took the vaccine cure ended up dying from lung failure. Once people were whole again and realized that the dead bodies of the victims of the Daze were piling up, they figured out there wasn't enough ground to bury all

111

the dead; the bodies were burned in mass fires. The stench of burning human flesh disturbed those who were immune, but no one got sick from it. However, and for those who had not received the vaccine cure, the smoke from it was toxic and they died."

"What happened to the governments?"

"Destroyed!" shouted Peter, making Doctor Bartholomew and I jump. We both gave him a dirty look and he chuckled to himself.

I answered, "They were crumbling and in disarray all over the world and in every country, there was either chaos or unity. The bureaucracies that had developed over centuries could no longer function. Institutional knowledge disappeared with every Dazed person that got locked out of reality. For North America, there was chaos. Everywhere you went, you would see cities burning to the ground – from mass sterilization fires that got out of control – and people wandering aimlessly. Some places fared better than others depending on climate and culture."

"Now, how was Arboria formed?"

"Since the northwest of the United States was where everything was centralized – the Daze, the vaccine cure, and Alexander Nicholls' investigation and declaration of the vaccine cure – we banded together. People in the northwest were used to a system of government that involved voting, so the people wanted a ballot concerning the future of our area. It was a difficult process, especially considering that everywhere had some level of chaos, so town hall meetings were done in every city and representatives were brought to Olympia, the capital of Washington State, to discuss and vote on what to do.

"The majority wanted a representative government, but also felt the need for leadership who could work beyond the bureaucracy to build and run the country as needed. For the most part, those who did not like the decisions made relocated to other parts of the

112

continent. The first King was selected by election and nearly everyone voted for Alexander Nicholls. He had done so much more than tell everyone about the vaccine cure; he also made decisions and led the people in many different ways up to that point."

I glance over at Peter, who was now staring at the blank wall behind Doctor Bartholomew as if it was actually an intricate, detailed work of art. I knew how he felt.

"He split the northwest into ten provinces and appointed new Nobility, Dukes and Duchesses, to each one. Every province voted for a representative, a Delegate, who would work with the Noble to make sure the people's voices were being heard. Every Province Delegate and Duke or Duchess was a part of the Council, who would regularly meet with the King for the same reason and to prevent the King from having too much power."

"Princess, you seem to have good knowledge of our history and how the kingdom is governed. I will let King Aaron know I have full confidence in you."

I furrowed my brow in confusion. "That is all? We are done? What about all the *other* things you have taught me?"

He waved off the question as if it was ridiculous. "I already know you know all that. I knew you knew what we discussed today, as well, but wanted to run through it one more time with you." I quickly interpreted all the "knows" and "knews" to decipher what he had said.

I rose and Peter followed my action. "Thank you, Doctor Bartholomew."

I expected him to just dismiss me, but he, instead, gave me his single clap of approval and rounded his desk to give me a deep bow. "It has been an honor, Your Highness."

Making eye contact with me, Peter shrugged and smiled before Doctor Bartholomew had brought himself back up to standing from his bow. I nodded once to him and left the tutoring room for the last time, thinking about the future ahead of me.

Chapter 15

Silently, Peter and I went to my rose maze from my tutoring session. When we got to the center, we sat on the sofa swing in the white gazebo. He sat first and I followed, leaning against him and allowing his arm to drape over my shoulders.

"Is everything alright, Rose?" He asked me.

"Hmm?" I had to shake myself out of my thoughts and concerns for my future. "Oh. Yes. Everything is fine, Peter." I turned around and gave him a smiling kiss, letting it linger. In acceptance, he pulled me closer and deepened the kiss, then withdrew his lips and rested his forehead against mine.

"You're not fine. I can tell it in your kiss. Plus, you are a *terrible* liar," Peter whispered.

Sighing, I breathed back, "You caught me." Separating our foreheads, I stayed close and looked him in the eyes. "I just don't know how you're going to react when I tell you what I think you should know."

Relaxing his embrace, he furrowed his brow and said, "Whatever you need to tell me, you can do it without worry. I love you too much."

I gasped and I am sure all the color left my face. "You *love* me?"

He laughed breathily. "Yes, Rose. I wasn't going to tell you unless I won the King's Test, but something tells me you should know now."

"We have been together for five years and you have never said anything that serious to me."

He shrugged. "Maybe it's time that I do."

I closed my eyes. "It complicates things, that's for sure. It kind of makes me even more afraid to tell you." Opening my eyes, I took a deep breath. "Remember this morning when I received the comm from Stephan?"

Peter quirked a brow and drawled, "Yes."

Looking down and biting the corner of my bottom lip, I just came out with it. "He was calling to inform me that I'm the only woman he wants to marry. He didn't say it, but between that and the other night in our interview and – kiss – it seems like he is in love with me."

Peter took in a sharp breath. "How long?"

"I'm not sure, but it sounds like it has been for a long time."

His embrace tightened again in frustration. "Why *now*?"

"Same as you. He said he couldn't go into the King's Test without telling me. He couldn't keep silent about it with the possibility of us being married in a few months."

"I'm going to kill him."

"Peter – "

He pressed a finger to my lips to prevent me from going any further. "Before you say he doesn't know anything about us, you should know that he *does.*"

As he brought his hand back around my waist, my eyes widened. "You *told* him?!"

"Well, *you* told Ella."

"I actually didn't. She guessed only yesterday. But that doesn't matter right now. Why would he do that when he knows how you feel about me? You're friends. You didn't know?"

"No. That's why I am mad. I can't believe he would betray me like this. He must have done it knowing he'd be late in arriving. Didn't want me getting a head start."

I laughed. "It's a bit late for that." Peter smiled, but didn't calm himself. I placed my hand on his cheek and he tilted his head into it. "Peter, you have nothing to worry about as far as *my* affections." I said it, but I wasn't sure if it was totally true.

Then, he relaxed. "I know. I suppose I should be grateful that the most likely person to win the test will love you."

I frowned. "Don't say things like that. You have just as much chance as he does."

He chuckled sardonically. "You and I both know that is not true."

Before I could stop it, a tear unexpectedly fell from the corner of my eye and my lower lip pouted without intention. Peter wiped the tear with his thumb. "Please don't cry, Rose," he begged.

"I can't help it. It's not fair that there's a possibility I can't marry a man that I choose." More tears began to fall and pretty soon

117

they were falling like a torrential downpour in October. He brought my head to his chest with his hand and stroked my hair in comfort.

Placing his cheek on the top of my head, he said quietly, "Shh. It's alright. We'll just have to take advantage of the time we're guaranteed together."

I nodded. We spent the rest of the day together either in the rose maze or sitting out in a field or walking through the forest. As much as I hated to admit it, Peter was right. Chances are, Stephan would win and I would have to marry him. Also, it was quite possible this would be the last week we could pull away alone. When Stephan arrived the next week, we were sure he would find every way conceivable to keep us apart.

The trouble was, I didn't know whether or not all that *really* bothered me.

Chapter 16

The next morning, Peter and I sat together at breakfast, but were silent. Food wasn't something I felt up to at the time and I pushed my eggs around my plate with my fork.

"What do you think, Rose?" I shook myself out of my stupor when I realized Father was addressing me.

"I'm sorry." I smiled. "I missed that. Could you repeat it?" Peter's hand that was under the table moved to my knee as if acknowledging he knew what was running through my head, which he was only partially right about.

"Is everything alright?"

"Yes, of course. I am just a little tired." It wasn't completely a lie. When Peter dropped me off at my room the previous night, I changed without Marie and went straight to bed. All I could think of was the circumstance Peter and I had created by being in a relationship. I was also upset not only about Stephan's confession and my own confusion, but his betrayal of Peter.

"Well, as I was saying, the Council was discussing the beginning of the King's Test and thought it would be a good idea for you to give a speech through the royal channel of the holocomm."

I nodded and shrugged. "I assumed that I would be doing that anyway. I have already begun composing it."

"Excellent. Please excuse me. I am sorry to leave before you are finished, darling, but your mother and I have some business to attend to." He held Mother's hand to help her stand and moved around behind my chair to kiss me on my cheek.

As they left, Peter leaned over and said, "I'm sorry, Rose."

I glanced over at Ella, silently asking if she could leave. Politely, Ella excused herself to give us a little privacy.

"What are you sorry for? You've done nothing wrong."

He shook his head. "I know. I'm just sorry *for* you because I'm somewhat experiencing what you're going through. It's so difficult for me. I can only imagine how you're feeling."

"How do you mean 'somewhat'?" I asked him.

He stood and helped me up holding my hand. Giving it a little squeeze before letting go, he led me out of the Dining Hall and down the stairs to go to our swing in the rose maze.

Sitting down, he held both my hands as I stood in front of him. "You are having to deal with the possibility of not only losing me, but being forced to marry without love at all. There is a chance that I might fall in love again and will be able to marry for love when all is said and done."

I frowned and took my hands slowly out of his. "You think you'll get over me that fast?"

He took both hands back quickly. "No. No, no, no. Not at all. That is *not* what I am saying." He let go and ran a hand through his short blond hair. "I don't know how to say what I'm trying to say."

I sat next to him and thought about what he had said. Shouldn't I *want* him to eventually marry for love? Wouldn't that be the loving thing to desire for him? Without looking at him, I held his hand sitting next to me on the swing and said, "I think I understand what you're saying."

He looked at me with those deep brown eyes that I loved so dearly, but I couldn't look at them. "Rose, I love you. You'll always have a place in my heart. There's nothing I can do about it and I'm not sure I would want to even if I could. But we'll both have to move on sooner or later."

Turning to me, he gently tipped my face to him, forcing me to look into his gentle gaze. "If there was anyone I would want you to be with aside from me, it would be Stephan. Even if he *wasn't* in love with you, I know he would take care of you. I want you to know, I won't be offended if you fall in love with him after you're married."

I closed my eyes and brought my hand over his own that was still on my cheek. "You make it sound like it's inevitable. Do you really have such little faith in yourself?"

While my eyes were still closed, he moved close to me and kissed me gently at first, but then transformed it into one of fervency. His hand traced my jaw and neck, and moved down to the small of my back, pulling me to him. I put my arms around his neck and made our kiss even more passionate.

As Peter ended our kiss, he kept us in our embrace and smiled. "That's one of the things I love about you, Rose. You have such an unreasonable faith in me."

I laughed. "Can't be helped. You haven't failed me yet. I see no reason for that to change now."

Smiling bigger and shaking his head, he stood up. "We should probably find Ella lest people become suspicious about all this time we have been spending alone." Peter wagged his eyebrows.

Sighing, I joined him. "I don't want to hear any more talk about the unknown future, though. Let's live in this moment."

He gave me a peck on the lips. "Alright. I think I can manage that."

~ ~ ~

We found Ella looking through a picture book of Britainnia we had recently acquired. When she heard the door slide open, she looked up at us and raised an eyebrow. "I'm surprised to see you two today."

Glaring at her as the door slid shut behind us, I said, "We figured we should spend time with you today to not provoke suspicion."

Ella laughed and I heard a muffled snigger come from Peter. Ella said, "That's what I figured. I just wanted to yank your roots a bit. No need to be so serious, Rose."

No sooner had she finished her teasing when the door slid open again behind us. Ella put her book down and Peter and I turned to see who it was. Father and Mother walked in.

Do they know? They look pretty upset...

Father said, "Oh good. I am glad all three of you are here. Peter and Miriam, please sit down."

They used my real name. They must know! I'm in so much trouble.

As Peter and I joined Ella on the sofa, Father and Mother sat on the sofa across from us. Father was stoic and Mother looked like she had been crying. Peter's leg started bouncing on its own volition and I was trying to be as still as possible.

"What's going on, Father?"

Unusual for him, he avoided eye contact by looking down at his hands folded in his lap. "This is not easy to say. It is a very – confusing situation."

I'm sure you are *confused, Father.*

"Father, I – "

"Please don't interrupt. I just need to be out with it. A very serious virus has been reported in all family members of the Cedar and Willow Noble houses. They've been quarantined until their illness can be determined not contagious."

As I started fidgeting with my fingers, Peter's leg stopped moving. I looked over to Ella, who looked back to me mirroring the same look of anxious uncertainty I was sure was on my face as well. Looking back to Father, I asked, "No one knows what the disease is? Not even Doctor Winston?"

"Darrel Winston doesn't even know. He has sent an assistant out to the Willow Province, since it is nearest to his lab here on the palace grounds, to get a sample of saliva he can test."

"But he *has* determined that the Cedars and Willows have the same thing? How can that be? They're virtually on different sides of the kingdom."

Father shook his head. "We know they have the same thing. Their symptoms are identical and have been progressing at the same rate over the last few days. Doctor Winston agrees with you that it is odd considering their distance. He has also pointed out that while the families have contracted the disease, none of the household staffs or guards have."

"Do you think maybe it was contracted at the King's Test Ball?"

"No. Neither does Doctor Winston. Apparently, some members of the households were exhibiting symptoms before the ball."

Bending over so my elbows rested on my knees and my head rested on my hands, I said, "Please let me know if the Council meets concerning it. This is the sort of thing I should have hands-on experience with so I can have more preparation for becoming Queen, aside from history and etiquette."

Father gave me a small smile, though it didn't reach to his eyes. "Alright, Miriam." He stood and gave Mother a hand in joining him. "Amoura, let's go back to my office and await updates." Looking back to me, he assured me, "We will keep you posted."

When they left the room, Ella moved to the couch they had been sitting on and Peter rested a hand on my back. We sat in silence for a few minutes, consumed with our thoughts.

How is this possible? What do the houses have in common? There hasn't been a gathering of the Nobility for quite some time before the King's Test Ball. I wonder what kind of symptoms they're having. I should have asked Father.

"The Cedar children are so young. The oldest isn't even ten yet," Ella broke the silence in the library.

I nodded. "The youngest is three. Theo's brothers, sister-in-laws, nephews and nieces are all under the same roof, too. I hope the symptoms aren't painful. I would hate to know they are suffering too much."

"Blossoms! Why didn't I think of asking?!" Ella vocalized the thoughts I had just been having.

"I was just thinking the same thing." I covered my face with my hands. "I'm going to be Queen someday. That's the sort of thing I should think of when a problem of this magnitude comes up." Peter's hand on my back began moving in circles.

"Don't beat yourself up too much, Rose. You're not Queen yet," Peter tried to comfort me.

"I could be, though. Anything can happen. My parents could die by any number of different ways and I would need to rule. I should be more prepared than this."

Silence fell again. What I said couldn't really be argued, though I did wish one of them would have said something about me being more prepared than I thought I was. I was supposed to be ready now. That was why our kingdom had the special Crowning Coronation when the heir to the Crown turned twenty-one.

While heirs in other kingdoms were accepted into adulthood, and even married off, by the time they were seventeen or eighteen, ours waited until twenty-one so the heir, and his or her spouse, could be more prepared and mature. If the King and Queen were to die before the heir was twenty-one, which had never happened up to that point, a Regent would rule until the heir was of age.

"I wonder if Count Theodore will be better by the time the King's Test comes around," Peter pondered aloud.

I took my face out of my hands and gave him a dirty look. "What? You can't blame me for wanting less competition," he reasoned.

"Plus, he's a lascivious scoundrel," Ella said. I shifted my dirty look to her and she shrugged.

125

I answered, "Even if he *is* still sick by the time the King's Test is supposed to begin, he wouldn't be disqualified. The Council would just postpone it until he was better." Peter sighed. "Besides, it's an unkind thing to say. We may not be close friends with him, or even *want* to be, but we *do* know him. You should be concerned, not filled with hope that he stays sick."

Peter slumped over at my chastisement, but moved his hand from my back to around my waist and pulled me closer to him. I still didn't sit up, but it was nice to feel his nearness.

"He won't win anyway," Ella pointed out thoughtlessly.

"Ella!"

She waved off the rebuke implied in the way I said her name. "This has nothing to do with him being or not being sick, Miriam, so save the lecture. I was simply stating a fact. He's not the sharpest knife in the drawer, no matter how handsome he is. Anyway, Uncle was about to order his execution the other day after what you told him happened in his interview." I widened my eyes at her.

"Wait. What happened the other night?" Peter asked as he straightened up again.

"Oh. You didn't tell him?" Ella asked, ashamed of bringing it up.

"No. I did not. It's official King's Test information. If I tell him and not the others, it is an unfair advantage," I snapped. Actually, I was really upset because I didn't want Peter worrying about any alone time I would have to spend with Theo during the test.

"I don't care if it gives me some kind of an advantage. Tell me, right now, Rose. What did he do?" Peter was angry and shouting at me. It wasn't something he had done before.

"Peter, calm down," I said.

"Not until you tell me!" he shouted.

"Fine! Just shush. Stop yelling at me."

Peter snapped his mouth shut, but he was breathing rapidly through his nose.

"He –" I stopped to think about how to put it for him. "In a nutshell, he got kissy and handsy very fast and offered to take my virginity gently that night."

Peter and Ella both looked at me with mouths gaping.

"Well, that's one way to put it," Ella said. "But it's accurate."

Peter turned to look at Ella now and she closed his mouth with her fingertip.

After a moment, Peter said, "If this illness doesn't kill Theo, *I* will."

"Peter!" I chastised.

Ella snickered.

"Can't blame me."

I shoved him playfully. "Yes, I can."

We spent the rest of the morning visiting in the library. Things lightened up after our conversation and we were soon reminiscing. Since Ella and I had known each other our whole lives, we had a lot more stories than those about us with Peter. However, he didn't mind hearing them. He was in hysterics by lunch time.

The three of us walked over to the Dining Hall to eat. Father and Mother weren't there, so I figured they were still sitting by the phone waiting in anticipation for updates concerning the Cedars and Willows. Because I hadn't received an update from them, I figured they hadn't heard anything yet.

We ate our lunch in relative silence with only brief comments about the food. When we finished, we went downstairs and out the door to the field of wild flowers. I made sure to have a Guard inform Father and Mother of my whereabouts so they could easily find me if something came up.

A few minutes after we made it out to the field, the same Guard came out to give me a message. Apparently, the samples had arrived for Doctor Winston to examine. Once again, our concern for the Cedars and Willows consumed our conversation before it turned lighthearted again.

Our afternoon was peaceful. We continued to reminisce, which turned into Peter and Ella teasing me about my being the Rose of Petrichoria.

"Rose arose to peruse the garden of roses." Peter said in an exaggerated Britainnian accent during his and Ella's tirade of teasing me.

I laughed. "Peter, 'peruse' doesn't contain the word 'rose' in it."

He looked at me indignantly. "Well – it sounds like it, so it counts." Ella was laying on her side with her arms folded over her stomach laughing harder than either Peter or me.

"It doesn't really, Peter." I pointed out.

Peter shrugged. "It kind of does."

They continued to poke fun as we made our way to the Dining Hall for dinner. Father and Mother were still not there, so we didn't feel the need for decorum. We laughed and teased each other all through dinner and remained in the Dining Hall long after the sun had set.

"So the salmon says to the anemone – " Peter's joke was interrupted by the sound of the sliding double doors. Father and Mother entered morosely and joined us at the table. Peter, Ella, and I looked at them with the same worried expression on all our faces.

I cleared my throat. "Is there news on the Cedars and Willows?"

It was Mother who spoke this time. "Yes."

I waited a few beats for more information, then probed. "What is it?"

Mother took my hand. "Miriam, the Cedars and Willows died about two hours ago."

Peter, Ella, and I gasped in shock. "At the same time? How is that even possible?"

"Their deaths were within minutes of each other." Mother furrowed her brow. "It is quite concerning."

Realization hit me like a ton of bricks. "This was an attack, wasn't it? Some kind of biological weapon."

Father responded, "That's what we're thinking, but we won't really know anything until Doctor Winston examines the bodies. They should arrive at his lab within the hour."

"He wasn't able to get anything from the sample his assistant got for him?"

129

"No. He said it wasn't a large enough sample. He was firing his assistant when we got the calls." Doctor Winston was always firing assistants. They could never meet his incredible expectations.

"So, we just sit and twiddle our thumbs until Doctor Winston can figure it out?"

Father exhaled exasperatingly. "Regrettably, yes. I wish there was something more to be done. We will soon need to decide on new households to receive the honor of dukedom, but that isn't something we're going to deal with right now."

"When was the last you heard from Doctor Winston?"

"About an hour ago."

I stood up. "I am going to go pay him a visit and see if there is anything I can do or if he has any news."

"Miriam – "

"Don't try to stop me with my real name, Father. This is not an argument you will win. I have just been sitting idly while everything is happening. If I am to be Queen someday, I need experience. I am going." Peter and Ella both smirked despite themselves. Mother covered her mouth to hide hers. Everyone knew the stature and tone of voice I used and they all knew just as well that I would, indeed, be winning the argument.

Father exhaled loudly. "Very well. Let me know if you learn anything."

Peter and Ella began to stand to follow me and I waved at them dismissively. "I need to do this myself. I will see you both later."

Chapter 17

I quickly made my way downstairs and out the door, Guard in tow and wielding a light stick. When I walked in, Doctor Winston was standing in front of a microscreen with his hands braced behind his head and furrowed brows.

Without speaking, I walked over and stood next to him with my hands folded in front of me. I didn't want to interrupt his thought process. I could see what he was seeing, but it meant nothing to me.

As he pinched the bridge of his nose, he breathed out a small grunt of exasperation, then gasped when he turned to leave his spot and saw me.

Apologetically, I put my hands out and said, "I did not mean to startle you. Are you alright?"

He tried to smile as he bowed respectfully, but didn't really succeed. "No. It is alright Princess Miriam. I was just deep in thought. What can I do for you?"

"I was just coming to ask you the same question."

" – I do not understand."

"Father told me about the deaths of the Cedars and Willows. You have been so hard at work. Is there anything I can do to assist you? I know I am not scientifically minded, but I thought maybe there was something else I could do for you."

"That is very – unexpected."

I looked down at my hands. "Maybe it is selfish, but I am just frustrated that all I can do is sit around and wait on news. I want to do something useful to the process, even if it is something mundane."

Doctor Winston chuckled. "I am sure there is something I can come up with. Are you sure, though? It is already very late and I am nowhere near done for the day. I am more than likely going to be pulling an all-nighter."

I nodded enthusiastically. "I am sure. Thank you, Doctor Winston."

"No. Thank *you*, Princess Miriam. However, I am going to need to insist that you call me 'Darrel' if you are going to be here. I cannot handle the title all night, especially from someone near my age and higher up the social ladder."

I scoffed. "The social ladder does not really mean much to me. Especially in a circumstance like this. Look at Father, Mother and I right now. We cannot get our own answers at this time and it is not fair for you to be the only one working on this all night.

"But I will make a deal with you. I will call you 'Darrel' if you will call me 'Miriam.' I do not think I can take the title all night either, especially from someone so near my age and more intelligent than me." I grinned at him.

He returned the smile. "I see what you did there. Alright. We have a deal."

Just then, his holocomm lit up and he answered it. The palace Steward's face appeared. "Hello, Steward. What can I do for you?"

"Princess Miriam has a comm from Count Stephan Oak. Is she available?" The Steward said, all business.

Darrel moved and gestured for me to go on over to the holocomm.

Thankfully, the Steward's face was still up when I walked over. "Thank you for the information, Steward, but please inform Stephan that I will be unavailable for most of the night."

He nodded and disconnected the comm. I moved to join Darrel, wide-eyed, across the room. When I was halfway there, the holocomm lit up again. Darrel answered it and it was the Steward again. We switched places.

"Yes, Steward?" I asked impatiently.

"I am so sorry to disturb you, Your Highness, but Stephan wanted me to ask that you comm him when you are finished, no matter what time it is."

I rubbed my eyes with the heels of my hands. "Let him know I will. Steward, please do not disturb me with anymore calls or questions this evening. Especially from any suitors. Just take messages and give them to me in the morning."

"Yes, Your Highness." The comm was disconnected again and I blew a lungful of air slowly through pursed lips.

"Prin – Miriam, you did not need to do that. You could have spoken to him."

I turned and looked at him. "I did not want to deal with it right now and it would have been rude for me to do so right after offering you my assistance."

He quirked an eyebrow, probably at my stating that I did not want to deal with my best friend. Affirming my assessment of his face, he said, "Not my business."

I laughed a breath. "No, it is not. Let us just say he is complicating things right now. So, what is it I can do for you? Have you eaten dinner?"

He had to think about it. "No. In fact, I have not eaten since breakfast."

Putting a hand on my hip and smirking, I responded, "Well, if you are going to last all night, you will need to eat something. Honestly, you are a doctor. You should know better than to skip meals. The cooks are done in the kitchen for the night, but I will walk over and get you something. I will be back in a bit."

Before he could stop me, I walked out with my light stick and my Guard again. I decided to jog to make it there faster. When I got to the kitchen, I threw together a chicken sandwich with some raw carrots, an apple, and a tall glass of water. After putting it all on a tray, I walked slowly back to his lab.

On my way out, I ran into Peter, literally, and almost dropped everything. Even though I knew it was partially my fault, I glared at him. "I'm sorry, Rose!" He looked at the tray. "What are you doing with all that food?"

"Doctor Winston hasn't eaten since breakfast, so I am bringing him some food."

He grabbed the tray, handed it off to a surprised Guard, then pulled me to him by my hips. "You've never brought *me* food. Should I be jealous?"

Irritated with his impertinence, but needing to go, I gave him a short kiss on his lips, escaped his embrace, and took my tray back from my grateful Guard, who smiled at me.

I am on a mission of great importance and I will not be swayed by the temptation of Peter this time.

"Of course you should be jealous. He's *much* brighter than you." I teased him with a wink and he laughed.

Peter placed his hand over his heart, "Rose, you wound me." Chuckling, he said, "I'll walk you to the door." He did and kissed me goodnight before I began walking back to Darrel's lab. Just as I was arriving, the freezer hover was as well.

My smile quickly fell from my face. I knew what was in the hover-truck. The door to the lab was open when I got there. As I walked in, I set the tray on a blank spot on his counter near the door and made my way over to the body that was laid out on the table. Darrel was having the others put into the waiting mortuary.

"Oh," I said softly when I got to the table. Sitting in the chair next to him, I brushed a lock of dark hair from Theo's damp face and my eyes filled with tears. Taking his cold hand in mine, I whispered to him as if he could hear me. "I'm so sorry, Theo. I wish I could have done something to help you. If it means anything now, I forgive you for the other night." I closed my wet eyes and kissed his forehead.

As I kissed him, my mind flashed to the image I had seen of the seven coffins. One disappeared. I straightened out abruptly and gasped at the event and the major headache that followed. Before that moment, I had never had a premonition while awake.

I jumped when Darrel came and stood next to me. He hesitated a moment, then put an arm around me awkwardly for comfort and said, "If this is too difficult for you, we can start with someone else."

I considered telling him what happened, but decided against it. I didn't need him worrying about me and the disease that took the Cedars and Willows, as well. Looking at him with my damp eyes, I swallowed and said, "I think this is going to be hard for me no matter who it is. I knew all of these people." After a pause, I added, "I placed your tray of food over by the door."

"I am afraid I have lost my appetite, but I might munch on it throughout the night."

I looked back at Theo. "What were his symptoms? Was it horrible for him?"

Nodding, he answered, "I wish I could tell you it was not horrible, but it was. By the sound of things, he died from a heart attack."

"But he was so young. We only just danced together a few nights ago."

"It is definitely a conundrum. I was told that it began with a slight headache and a slightly increased heart rate. By the end, he was delusional and sweating profusely as a result of his rapid heart rate."

I furrowed my brows and stepped out of his arm. Leaning against a nearby counter, I noted, "It sounds almost like Oramatosis, but that is not possible, right?"

He laughed dryly. "Right. Look, Miriam. I am very grateful for you coming down here and offering me help, but I think it might be best if you go to your room and turn in for the night. I do not think this will be good for you."

"You are right. I am sorry I could not be of more assistance, Darrel. Please let me know anything you find out."

He took my hand and helped me stand. Escorting me to the door, he said, "Thank you for the food and again for offering assistance."

"You are welcome," I answered numbly and walked as if in a trance to my room on the fifth floor of the palace.

Chapter 18

Staring at my ceiling, I thought about everything I had just witnessed. I honestly had not expected to see Theo that way. I couldn't help remembering all the time we had laughed together – before I learned what he wanted from me. He was a great dancer.

Was. I can't help wondering how he would have fared in the King's Test. Not well, probably. He definitely wouldn't have made it to the final two with Stephan. Oh! Stephan!

I had completely forgotten that I told him I would comm him no matter the time. Glancing at my clock, I sighed when I saw it was 1:00 AM. After rising and stretching, I walked over to my holostation and commed him.

"Rose? Is that you?" He was squinting at me and looked disheveled. He ran a quick hand through his hair.

"I'm sorry, Stephan. I know it's late, but the Steward told me to comm you back no matter the time. Did he give me the wrong message?"

Stephan rubbed his eyes with his fingers and yawned. "No. No. He gave you the right message. I've just been having a little headache and decided to take a nap before you called."

My eyes widened. "A headache? How's your heart rate?"

He laughed. "I don't know. I haven't been checking it."

"I'm sorry. I got back from Doctor Winston's lab about an hour ago and it was disturbing."

"Why were you with Doctor Winston?"

"I was tired of sitting around doing nothing when such a strange disease was taking residence with the Cedars and Willows and God knows who else."

"Yeah. I heard about that. So weird. I wonder if Count Theodore will be better by the King's Test."

My bottom lip began trembling and I looked down. "Both the Cedars and Willows died this evening within minutes of each other."

There was silence between us for a few moments. "They're *dead*?" Stephan asked.

Tears started to fall again despite my trying to stop them and I looked back at him. "Yes. Doctor Winston still doesn't know what's going on. The samples he took earlier when they were still – alive – weren't adequate for proper testing. He's thinking he'll know more once he performs the autopsies."

"Trees and Blossoms. Is that why it was disturbing for you? Did you see one of the bodies?"

Nodding, I choked a response. "Yes. I saw Theo. Doctor Winston hadn't closed his eyes yet and his hair was over his face like it was when he danced. His face and hands were so cold and damp."

"I'm so sorry you had to see him like that. I know he was one of your favorites to dance with at balls."

140

Sniffling, I changed the subject. "What was it you wanted to talk to me about?"

Stephan shrugged. "Nothing really. I just wanted to talk with you. I felt like we left things kind of – awkward last night."

I scoffed. "Yeah. Just a little. Why didn't you tell me that you knew about Peter and me?"

His jaw dropped. "You told Peter?"

"Of course I told Peter. I figured he should know given that the King's Test isn't far away."

Stephan slapped his hand on his face. "How did he react?"

"His exact words were 'I'm going to kill him.' He felt pretty angry with what he referred to as your 'betrayal'."

"I wish you would have told me you were going to tell him." He was mad, but keeping a calm face. I didn't have the patience to match his calm.

"I didn't know that Peter had told you about us! How was I supposed to know that?!"

Stephan put his hands up in front of him as a sign of surrender. "You're right. You're right. I'll just have to talk with Peter when I get there." There was another pause in our conversation.

Quietly, he said, "Rose, I know you're not in love with me. I even know you're probably having a difficult time facing the possibility of marrying anyone besides Peter. If I don't make it to the end, I hope he does; there isn't anyone else I'd trust to make you happy."

"He said something very similar about you earlier."

"Well, at least there's that. I'm sure I've upset the balance in our friendship by telling you how I feel, that I love you, but I can't control that."

He said it.

"Even if I hadn't told you, the balance would be off; it has been for some time now. I have talked with my parents, who were *not* happy when I told them what I told you, and they've agreed to release me from the commitment I made to them to stay home another week. Seems like they don't want you stewing on it too long with Peter there alone. I'll be at Evergreen Palace at around noon."

I gulped. "This is a lot to take in."

"That's why I think I should come up now rather than later. I think the anticipation and anxiety waiting will only make things tenser between us."

"You're probably not wrong." I laughed quietly. "I've got to go now, Stephan. I need to sleep. Good night."

"Good night, Rose. I'll see you later."

Relieved that he disconnected first, I went back to my bed and pulled myself into the blankets. Closing my eyes, I thought about the situation with Stephan. I knew why it consumed my thoughts, but I didn't want to acknowledge it. It was too much to bear that a part of me felt the same way for him.

I loved Peter, but I also loved Stephan. Knowing I needed to make a decision even if a relationship wouldn't necessarily last because of the King's Test, I decided to break things off with Peter so I could make a choice.

Having decided what I needed to do that day, I quieted my mind and focused on the rain pelting on the roof above me to ease myself into sleep.

I sit in my treehouse in the middle of the forest after learning about the King's Test. At thirteen, I now know I will not be permitted to marry for love and have been expressly forbidden from pursuing romance before the King's Test in eight years.

I think about the gentlemen who will be participating. Because they are all older than me, they all know already. I'm unfamiliar with Brian and Christopher. Theo is a good dancer and is awfully cute. Peter seems arrogant, so I try to ignore him as much as possible.

Leonard and Lincoln's mother is friends with mine and every so often I have to endure their obnoxious presences. Luckily, Mother never makes me entertain them alone, though I wonder whether that is a mercy or protection on her part.

What hurt to find out was that Stephan will be a participant and has known about the King's Test for years; he never even hinted at it. We have always been so close. I love him like a brother and it confuses me that he would keep something so big from me.

"Rose?" I hear from the bottom of the tree. "Are you up there?" I would recognize Stephan's voice anywhere.

"Go away, traitor!" I yell down at him. "I don't want to talk to you!"

The sounds of a breathy chuckle and feet scrambling up the ladder tell me he has ignored me. The weed. When he pulls himself up to find me sitting in my glassless window, he crosses his arms.

"Why so sad, Princess?" Stephan asks, knowing I hate when he uses my title.

"Don't call me that, Count," I mumble, "and don't pretend like you don't know. Father sent you out here didn't he?"

Stephan unfolds his arms and comes over to sit next to me. "Yes, he did."

"Did you know?" I ask, even though I know the answer.

"Yes, I did," he sounds like he feels bad. Good. He should feel bad.

Turning watery eyes to meet his gaze, I ask, "Why didn't you tell me? How could you keep this from me?"

"I'm so sorry, Rose. I had no choice. I was forbidden and I had to promise not to tell you. The King said if I didn't promise not to tell you, I wouldn't be able to see you again until you found out from him. That would have been four years."

My eyes widen at the news. I can't believe Father made such a threat. Wait. Yes, I can. Tears begin flowing freely and I cover my face with my hands. "Oh, Rose," Stephan murmurs and pulls me into a hug. Stroking my hair, he comforts me.

"What if I have to marry Leonard or Lincoln? I don't think I can live with Leonard's annoying tick or Lincoln's bragging for my whole life."

"I won't let that happen."

I look at him again. "Promise?"

Stephan smiles big. "I promise I will at least do better than Leonard and Lincoln, Rose."

~ ~ ~

144

I woke up at around 10:00 AM that morning from my memory to the sound of knocking at my door. Before I could get up, I saw Marie get up off the sofa to answer. I must have been worn out because I didn't even hear her enter.

"Good morning, Marie. Is Princess Miriam awake?" I heard Peter at the door and groaned.

Before she could answer, I sat up and called out to them with slurred words. "I'm awake! Marie, you can take a break for a bit." She grabbed a green satin robe from my closet, handed it to me, and left the room.

As I stood up, I put the robe on and walked to the door to welcome Peter in. He smiled, came in, and sat on my sofa. Sitting down next to him, I folded my hands in my lap and looked down at them. "Stephan is going to be here around noon today."

Seemingly oblivious to how I was feeling, he lifted my chin and kissed me with zeal, clearly ignoring my morning breath. Wrapping his arms all the way around my back, he pulled me in as close as he could. As he dipped me against the arm of the sofa and threaded his fingers into my hair, I returned the kiss with the same passion he showed me. Tears began to drip from the corners of my eyes and down the sides of my head. Stopping the kiss, he kept his face close, looking into my eyes and still stroking my hair.

"I know, Rose. I know."

I inhaled sharply, trying to breathe normally. "What?" I asked without success to control my breathing.

Peter tilted his head. "I know that you're going to break up with me now."

My eyes widened. "How could you possibly know that?"

"I understand the way your mind works. When you told me about Stephan's affections, I could see the turmoil in your eyes. You're not the kind of person to be in a relationship with someone if he can't have your full heart and you have feelings for Stephan, too.

"There's also the fact that I've told you I love you several times since arriving here and you've never returned a similar statement."

Still rapidly breathing and a quicker heart, I tried to speak. "I – How – I never said I didn't."

Peter nodded. "I understand. But I can see you have strong emotions for Stephan and you may love him, too. I thought we would have more time. I felt that when he arrived, it would be over for us."

"But I still have feelings for you. I'm so confused right now."

Kissing my forehead and releasing me, he said, "Again, I know. You do not need to be sorry, Rose. I will always love you, just like I said yesterday." Without another word, he stood up and left me laying on my sofa completely dumbstruck.

Turning to face the back of my sofa and mourning my relationship with Peter, I let my tears freely fall. Incomprehension swept through me; on the one hand, I was so sad to end things with Peter. On the other, I was relieved that I would have the opportunity to feel things out with Stephan without thinking I was betraying Peter.

Marie came back in after a while to help me get ready for the day. I confided in her about what had been going on. Although she was my assistant, I also counted her among my friends. After I was done explaining, she gave me a big hug and suggested a nice, hot shower.

While I showered, she chose a dark brown A-line, halter top dress with ivory roses lining the hem. When I got out, she helped me get into my dress and quickly applied my everyday makeup. She also put my long, black hair in a simple ivory ribbon to keep it down, but out of my face. Forgetting to choose shoes for me, she left. I didn't mind.

As I walked into my closet to look at my selection of shoes, I heard my door slide open and close without invitation. Stepping out, I saw Ella trying to find me.

"Ella?"

"Rose? I saw Peter wandering the rose maze and he said I should come up to see you. What is going on?"

I sighed and moved back into the closet. It had become easier to breathe as I slowly calmed down after Peter left. "I broke up with Peter."

"What?!"

"Well, technically, *he* broke up with me, but I was going to do it anyway. I couldn't stay in a relationship with him because – I might share Stephan's affections. I still love Peter, but I can't be in a relationship with him if I can't give him everything." I shrugged. "I was going to have to end things eventually anyway."

Turning around, I selected a pair of ivory ballet flats. Slipping them on, I watched Ella as she joined me in my closet. When I was done and standing straight, she hugged me. "I am so sorry, Rose. This has to be hard for you."

Gently separating us, I said, "Yes and no. Yes, it rots that I had to end things with Peter sooner than I anticipated. No, because now I can explore whatever is going on with Stephan when he gets here at noon without a sense of disloyalty consuming my mind."

147

"Noon? Today?"

"Yes."

"Rose, you haven't been paying attention to the time. It's 12:30 right now."

"Why didn't you say something?!"

"I didn't know you were expecting Stephan today!"

We were interrupted by the sound of someone pressing the door chime to my room. "Yes?" I called out.

"It's me, Stephan. Can I come in?"

Quietly, I said to Ella, "You need to go. I'll fill you in later." Giggling, she let me push her to the door. Her girly giggles drove me crazy sometimes. It also drove me crazy how she could switch from being concerned to absurd at the flip of a coin.

Taking a deep breath, I answered the door. Stephan was clearly surprised to see both Ella and me in my room. Evidently, he had spent some time getting ready to see me; he looked handsome. His simple outfit of dark brown slacks and a snug button-up forest green shirt did wonders on him. I wondered how I had never noticed how good-looking he was before that moment. "Oh. I didn't know you were with Ella right now. I can come back later."

"No, that's ok. I was just leaving. I'll see you two later." She waved with her fingers as she left and Stephan chuckled at her silliness.

Fickle Ella.

I stood aside and gestured for him to enter. My chest ached and stomach turned – in a good way – and it made me even more confused. As the door slid shut behind me, I leaned back against it. Stephan turned around only a couple feet away from me. With his grey-green eyes looking into mine, he said, "I ran into Peter when I was trying to find you in the library."

"Oh. You did?"

Stephan took a step closer. "He told me what you did and why you did it."

"He did it, but I was going to," I corrected.

Why did Peter tell Ella and Stephan that I broke up with him?

I couldn't look away from Stephan's gaze.

Trees and Blossoms. I love him, too. What is wrong with me that I didn't realize it sooner?

"So, he told you I broke up with him because I have feelings for both of you?" I asked, inwardly grimacing with embarrassment for some reason.

He shrugged. "Well, *he* said you broke up because you're not sure if you are in love with either one of us, but I suppose it's all semantics." He took another small step forward and hesitantly took one of my hands in his.

"Right. Semantics."

I'm down to one-word phrases now. Great. He just kissed me the other night. Why am I nervous? Because everything is different now. That's why. And now I am rambling in my head.

He laughed breathily. "You don't need to feel nervous with me, Rose. I'm still the same person." He pulled me closer to him; we were now only a few inches apart.

149

He knows I'm nervous. Of course he knows. He knows me.

I swallowed hard. "Yes, but now I have tingles running up and down all over me at the very sight of you."

Did I just vocalize that?! Shut up! Shut up! Shut up!

"Is that so?" Stephan smirked and put a hand around my waist and pulled me in the rest of the way.

Don't shut up. Answer him.

I still couldn't turn my gaze away from his, though his eyes said so many things he had never told me until two days ago. "Yes? I mean – yes."

Letting go of my hand, he brought his up and traced the edge of my face with it. Tilting his head, he said, "You are so beautiful, Rose. I love everything about you from your bright green eyes to your soft heart." He brought his face within an inch of mine and looked at my lips.

He's going to kiss me. He's going to kiss me outside tradition and I'm going to let him. And I'm excited for it. I hope it's more than a peck. I hope he ravishes me. Ravishes? Do people even say that anymore? Does that mean what I think it means or something more than what I want? I know what I want. I want Stephan to kiss me. I'm rambling in my head again...when did that start happening? When Stephan threw me for a loop. That's when.

I bit the corner of my bottom lip and could only stutter, "Th – Thank you. You're beautiful, too. Handsome. I mean, handsome." I closed my eyes in self-mortification.

When did I become a stuttering fool like this? I was never like this with Peter. Of course, we were together nearly as long as we

150

knew each other. I've never been in a situation like this with Stephan. Not on our own, at least.

He misinterpreted the closing of my eyes and brushed his lips against mine tentatively. I could feel him smile in his kiss and swallow. I involuntarily mimicked his swallow. Cradling my head, he gave me a deeper, but still gentle kiss. My knees weakened beneath me and I could barely stay standing. As he pulled me in closer and supported my weight, I felt him sigh and I shivered. I couldn't resist reciprocating by putting my hands around his neck and bringing him as close as I could.

Yes. This is what I wanted.

I'm not sure how long we stood there kissing and holding onto each other, allowing ourselves to explore each other's heads, necks, backs, waists and hips in a way we had never even considered before; all I knew was that it felt right. It didn't feel like something I needed or wanted to hide. It wasn't a secret to be kept. It wasn't silly or frivolous. It was real and I never wanted it to end.

At that moment, I could clearly see that I was a mess of perplexity. I thought my feelings for Peter were the strongest I would ever feel, but then, in Stephan's arms, I felt the same strength, different as it may be. With Peter, it was a passionate love. With Stephan, I felt the years of companionship that built up to that point in time; to the moment of our first *real* kiss.

When he finally stopped our kiss, I opened my eyes and smiled at him. Stephan smiled in relief back to me. "You have no idea how long I have wanted to do that."

I giggled.

Did I seriously just giggle?

"How long?" I asked breathlessly.

"Hmm." He spent a moment calculating; I could see it in his expression. "Ten years, give or take a few months."

With wide eyes, I said, "Ten years?! You've been in love with me for a decade and you never said anything? That's longer than I've even *known* Peter. We could have had so much longer together if you had said something."

Stephan chuckled. "I was fifteen, Rose. What is a fifteen-year-old boy supposed to do with emotions like this? Scratch that. What is an eleven-year-old *Princess* supposed to do with such a declaration of love? You were so much younger than me. My parents had been trying to convince me it was alright because I might marry you someday, but I didn't know what to do.

"Over the years, it became more difficult. I knew you were not allowed to fall in love, but I wanted to court you. I wanted to hold you and kiss you like this, but I was too afraid to break the rules. When Peter told me about you two, I was furious at him *and* myself that he had the guts to do what I had been afraid to do for so many years.

"But I swear to you, Rose. From now until my dying breath I will love you and cherish you and be the man you need me to be. I am *that* confident that I will be your husband and King."

I was dumbstruck at his avowal to me. Smiling, I put my cheek against his chest, tucking my head in the crook of his neck. Embracing me a little tighter, he rested his chin there. "Still, you could have said something at some point."

He chuckled and turned his head so his cheek was pressed into my hair. "I'm saying it *now*. And you know I am probably more prepared than anyone else for the King's Test. This could be forever in only a few short months."

I took a deep breath. "That's a possibility I wouldn't be opposed to, Stephan Oak." Then, I took my turn and kissed him.

Chapter 19

In the next moment, Stephan's eyes glassed over and his arms went limp, causing me to fall to the floor. "Rose! I'm sorry! I'm not sure what came over me. It was like I was somewhere else for a moment."

Realization hit me like lightening. "No." It was all I could vocalize.

No. No, no, no. Please don't have whatever the Cedars and Willows had.

Stephan bent over and helped me up. "What's wrong? You look like you're going to be sick."

I shook my head. "I think we need to take you to see Doctor Winston."

"Why?"

I swallowed, though my mouth was dry and felt a sharp pain running through me. Putting a hand to his cheek, I explained, "Stephan, you're having the same symptoms the Cedars and Willows had."

His eyes became huge. "What?"

"I don't want to stand here having this discussion. We can talk about it with Doctor Winston."

Grabbing his hand, I pulled him out the door and down the stairs. I held tight, not caring who saw. It was all I could do to stop the tears from coming up. When we entered Darrel's lab, I didn't even care that I was interrupting his autopsy on Duchess Elizabeth Cedar.

"Darrel. I need you to stop what you're doing immediately and help me."

He slowly lowered his scalpel and lifted his glasses to the top of his head. Briskly walking to me, he said, "What is going on Princess Miriam?"

"This isn't the time for titles, Darrel. Stephan is having the same symptoms as the Cedars and Willows."

As his jaw dropped, his holocomm started beeping with an incoming comm. He quickly shook himself and went to answer. It was Father.

"Doctor Winston, I have some news."

Darrel pinched the bridge of his nose where his glasses normally sat. "Let me, guess, Your Majesty. The Oaks are having the same symptoms as the Cedars and Willows."

Hesitantly, Father drawled, "Yes. And the Junipers. – How did you know?"

Oh! Poor Peter!

"Because Princess Miriam just brought Count Stephan to my lab. He is exhibiting similar symptoms to the Cedars and Willows."

"I did not realize he had arrived." He paused. "Can you bring Princess Miriam over to the holocomm and give us a moment?"

"Yes, Your Majesty." Darrel gestured for me to come over.

"Hello, Father." I said, still trying to hold back my tears. "Is Peter sick, too?"

"No, but he's very angry that I won't let him go home." Quietly he asked me, "How long has Count Stephan been here?"

"I'm not sure. He was in my room for quite some time, though." I bit the corner of my lower lip and gave Stephan a sidelong glance.

Father quirked a brow. "Is there something you would like to tell me?"

Looking down at my fiddling hands, I said, "I think if you are planning on quarantining Stephan, you should probably quarantine me as well."

"Because you have been with him? It would be quite an undertaking to quarantine everyone who has had contact with Stephan since he's been here."

"Everyone hasn't had the same contact I have had with him." I sighed. "Father – we were kissing in my room when he glassed over and dropped me on the floor." I looked at the two gentlemen in the room with me for a moment and saw that both their faces were pale.

Face in hands, Father said, "Oh, Miriam." He sat like that for a moment, then slid his hands down his face. "Alright. Bring Doctor Winston back."

"Yes, sir." Darrel and I switched places again and I walked into an embrace with Stephan. He stroked my hair. I felt guilty; he was the one probably dying and he was comforting me.

157

"Doctor Winston, please put Count Stephan and Princess Miriam in the quarantine room until you have both tested their blood and concluded your examinations on the Cedars and Willows."

"Yes, Your Majesty. I am just about finished. I have a theory, but I do not want to say anything until it is conclusive. I will take a blood test from Count Stephan, as well. Even though he is not displaying symptoms, I would like Count Peter to be sent down for testing and quarantine, too."

Without another word, Father nodded and disconnected the comm. Darrel turned to look at us. Having given up holding back the tears, I was in deep sobs in Stephan's arms and he had his cheek on the top of my head as he continued to stroke my hair. Darrel nodded solemnly like he had a difficult task to perform even though he didn't want to do it.

Clearing his throat, he made his requests. "Very well, Count Stephan, please come have a seat in the Drawing chair. I will draw from you first, then Princess Miriam." We let go of each other and neared Darrel. Stephan sat first and put his wrist in the blood drawing cuff. The device hummed as it searched for a good vein and he winced when it found one and quickly drew three tubes of blood for Darrel to examine.

When it shut down, Stephan took his wrist out and we switched places. Because Darrel only needed one tube from me, the cuff was quicker for me and we were soon being led down a hall to the quarantine room.

Stephan went in first and I followed. Before the door slid shut, Darrel grabbed my wrist and pulled me back in the hall. "She will be with you in a moment," he assured Stephan, then closed the door.

"What is it, Darrel?" I asked him.

His glasses were still on top of his head and he instinctively itched the bridge of his nose. "I feel I should tell you my theory."

Furrowing my brow, I responded, "But, you just told Father that you did not want to tell until you were sure."

"I am fairly certain. I just did not want to say anything official." He took a deep breath. "Do you remember last night when you said the symptoms almost sounded like Oramatosis, then we both dismissed it?"

"Yes – Wait – Are you telling me it *is* the Daze?"

He nodded solemnly again. "Yes. And I am afraid the original vaccine cure will not work this time. It is a modified version in which it only targets a certain bloodline."

"So – you are also telling me this is a biological weapon? Someone is targeting *families*?"

"My theory is that they are not just targeting families, they are targeting *Noble* families."

I hesitated with my next question. "Are the Oaks and Junipers as good as dead, then?"

"I am afraid so. If anyone will survive, it will be Stephan and Peter. I have Stephan's sample and will soon have Peter's. I can begin on a cure for Stephan right away.

"Also, we probably do not need to worry about you having caught it, since it appears to be family-specific, but I will still test your blood anyway. You should not have to be in quarantine too long."

"You will be putting Peter in with us?"

"At least for now until I can clear him."

"Even if I am cleared, I will be staying. If Stephan is going to die, he is not going to do it alone."

Peter will understand. He must. We can comfort each other when it's all over.

"It will not be easy. When I get back my results, we will probably need to strap him to the table in there to prevent him from hurting himself or you. And it may be a good decision to sedate him if it gets too bad."

"Alright. I think I will go in the room now."

Darrel pushed the button that opened the door and I walked in. Stephan was sitting on the edge of the bed that had straps attached to it. "I wonder what these are for," he pondered out loud, holding one in his hand.

"Oh, Stephan," I cried as I quickly went over and knelt before him. Taking his hands, I explained everything Darrel had just told me. When I was finished, he looked into my wet eyes and placed a hand to my cheek.

"You should go, Rose. I don't want you to see me like that."

I shook my head with fervor. "I am not leaving you to die alone in here. Maybe it's selfish, but I want to have as much time with you as I can and I can't bear the thought of you being alone in here with your nightmares."

Wiping the tears from my cheek with his thumb, he leaned forward and kissed me. "I love you, Rose. No matter what you see here or what I become, please remember that I love you."

I pulled myself up to sit on the edge of the bed next to him and kissed him back. Stephan wrapped his arms around me and brought me close to him. Things became intense pretty fast as he moved away from my mouth and down my jawline to my neck. I never stopped crying. He came back to my lips and nibbled on my bottom lip. Without any warning, he bit it – hard – drawing blood.

"Ow!" I yelled. He had separated our faces and was looking past me. Making our embrace as tight as possible, he looked past me and at me at the same time as if I was something terrible.

Peter came in and quickly assessed he situation. He ran over and tried to pry Stephan off me.

"No! I can't let you out into the world!" Stephan screamed in my face. He flung one arm back and sent Peter across the room, then squeezed me again.

Crying harder, I desperately pushed at him, trying to get him to release me. "Stephan! Stephan! Wake up!" I was screaming at him.

He has *to wake up. This is too soon!*

As suddenly as he had turned on me, I felt his gaze come back into focus, though I wasn't looking at him. He was no longer looking at me angrily, but he hadn't let go. Looking down to my bottom lip, he paled. "Rose? Rose?"

I had my face turned away, but was looking at him in my peripheral vision. Slowly, I turned back and looked directly at him. He looked horrified as he took in the fact that I had a mixture of blood and tears streaming from the corner of my mouth down my neck and into my dress.

Peter slowly walked toward us.

161

Bringing a shaking hand to my mouth, Stephan said, "Please, tell me I didn't do this."

Though I didn't want it, a squeak escaped me.

"Rose, I'm so sorry." He began to cry himself, let me go, and stood to walk to the other side of the room, noticing Peter for the first time.

"Peter," Stephan said.

"Princess Miriam, is everything alright in there? Do you need help?"

I looked to the corner of the ceiling where Darrel's voice had sounded. There was a camera and speaker there.

"Everything is fine, Darrel. Things are just progressing more quickly with Stephan than either of us had anticipated," I replied.

"No! Everything is not fine, Rose! I *bit* you and *scared* you out of your mind! You need to leave before I seriously injure you!" Stephan screamed.

"Rose, I think Stephan is –" Peter began.

Standing, and ignoring Peter, I yelled back at Stephan. "I am *not* leaving you, Stephan!" I walked over and stole his hands into mine, even though he tried to pull away. Softer, I said again, "I am *not* leaving you. That isn't what someone who loves someone else does. I might have vowed to be with you in 'sickness and health, 'til death do us part' if life had allowed it and I am promising you that now. I will not leave your side until you have drawn your last breath."

Clearly mortified with himself, he tried to speak, but it ended up being more of a whisper, "Rose – "

"No, Stephan. Stop trying. Would you leave me if our roles were reversed?"

He took a deep breath in defeat. "No. I wouldn't." After a pause, he said, "Fine. I'll let you stay, but I want you to strap me down so I can't hurt you. I *would* do that for you."

Peter looked horrified and hurt.

"Everything alright, now?"

"Yes, Darrel. Everything is alright now," Stephan said.

Stephan took my hand and led me over to the bed, where he lay down and waited. As difficult as it was, I strapped his arms while Peter strapped his legs down and sat on the edge of the bed next to him. Placing one hand on his other side, I looked down at his face, wondering to myself how much longer Stephan would be Stephan.

Trying to pretend like Peter wasn't in the room, I bent down to kiss Stephan and he interrupted by saying, "Stop." I did and hovered only a few inches from his face. "What if I hurt you again?"

Biting the sore already forming on my lower lip, I said quietly, "I'll just give you a little peck. Last one. I promise. I don't want my last memory of your kiss being one where you were not you."

Waiting for his approval, I stayed there and watched him think about it. After he nodded, I slowly filled the gap between us. Though the kiss was short, it was far from a peck. I pulled us apart and lay my head on his chest. Closing my eyes, I listened to his increasing heartbeat.

"Can you rest on my shoulder? I would like to rest my cheek on you." Stephan asked.

I made eye contact with Peter and mouthed *"I'm sorry."* He nodded and mouthed back, *"I understand."*

Already in the process of bringing myself up a little higher, I said, "Of course." I closed my eyes. After a while, the men apparently thought I had fallen asleep.

"Peter?" Stephan asked.

"Count Peter? Your tests came back negative. You are free to go."

"Thank you. I'll leave in a bit," Peter addressed the speaker as he moved to sit next to Stephan and I on the bed. "What is it, friend?"

"I'm sorry," Stephan said.

"No. You don't need to be."

"Yes. I do. I shouldn't have betrayed you. I should have never told Rose I loved her."

"Yes, you should have. If you didn't, she would have never known."

"Would that have been so bad?" I felt a hand begin running fingers through my hair and knew it was Peter. Stephan continued. "Look at her. How sad she is. Do you think she would still be this sad if I had never told her?"

"Yes. You are her best friend. Even before you told her you were in love with her, she loved you as a brother."

There was silence for a moment. Peter broke it. "If there would be anyone to marry Rose besides me, I would have wanted it to be you." Another pause happened.

"Promise me you'll take care of her," said Stephan

"I can't promise that I'll win the King's Test. There are more qualified men, even without –" Peter didn't finish his thought, but Stephan did.

"Me. I don't necessarily expect you to. What I want is for you to promise me you will take care of her regardless of the results of the King's Test. Protect her. Make sure whoever she ends up with knows there will always be someone watching out for her."

"I promise. And I'll comfort her when you're gone."

"She'll be there for you, too." Stephen chuckled dryly. "Probably more so than you will be for her, no offense. It is just her personality to give everything, even if she has nothing to give. I'm sorry about your family."

Pause. "They died shortly before I came in here. King Aaron won't let me leave to bury them."

"I'm so sorry. Why haven't you said anything before now?"

"I don't want to worry Rose. She's dealing with enough right now with you and the King's Test and everything else the world is throwing at her."

"Thank you, Peter." Pause. "I love you, brother."

"Love you, too, Stephan."

He bent over us and gave Stephan a hug, then said goodbye and left.

Not long after, I felt Stephan's breathing regulate and knew he was asleep for possibly the last time. With a deep sigh, I joined him, wishing we could dream together.

~ ~ ~

"Ahhhhhhhhhh!" I woke to Stephan screaming in my ear and I jumped up off the bed. His eyes were open and moving as quickly as if he was deep in REM sleep. "HELP! HELP! ROSE! NO! DON'T HURT HER!"

"I'm alright, Stephan! I'm right here! No one is going to hurt me!" I was screaming over him to no avail. Knowing he wouldn't be overcoming his nightmare this time, I began weeping uncontrollably and fell to my knees.

Darrel ran in with a syringe and gave Stephan whatever medication was in it. Both of us had assumed a sedative would calm him down, but it only seemed to make things worse. The veins in his neck were raised as he screamed in fear not for his own life, but for mine.

Shaking his head, Darrel walked over to me and placed a comforting hand on my shoulder. There was nothing to be done. We waited for probably an hour, listening to Stephan screaming and ranting before a literal deathly silence fell on the room.

Slowly, I stood up and approached the bed. Stephan's grey-green eyes and mouth were wide open. I closed his eyelids, then his mouth. Quietly, I unstrapped him, then left the room, Darrel following close behind me.

Without stopping or turning to look at him, as I walked out the door, I said, "I will leave you to your work, Darrel."

Chapter 20

Having just loved and lost in the same day, I was in a state of bewilderment. I don't even remember how I got there, but somehow, I made it to the swing in the center of my rose maze. The moon was full and bright. It was a small comfort knowing that we had been asleep for quite a long time before Stephan lost it completely.

Sitting sideways, I leaned against an arm of the sofa swing and pulled my knees into my chest. As I wrapped my arms around my knees, I put my head on them and closed my eyes. Much earlier in the day, I had lost the ivory ribbon Marie had tied so beautifully in my hair and my long black tresses fell over my face. For only a moment, the image of the coffins appeared again and another wooden coffin disappeared. Another headache throbbed. By that point, it was clear what the coffins meant: six of the seven participants of the King's Test were going to die, probably from this mutated Daze. How I wished I could cry, but my eyes refused to allow any more tears to fall.

"Rose?"

When I heard him say my name, I could hear the croak in Peter's voice, probably from his own crying. His family was dead and he lost Stephan, too. Stephan's family would probably be gone soon, if they weren't already, assuming the pattern followed what happened with the Cedars and Willows.

Looking up and at him, I saw the tell-tale signs of someone who had just spent a long time crying: puffy eyes, red nose, flush cheeks. I was sure I didn't look much different.

"Hello, Peter," I croaked.

"Is he gone?"

I nodded.

"Would you mind if I sat with you? I know it's late and you have had a long day."

I gave him a small smile. "I'm sure you have, too. Please sit."

He sat down next to me and laid his head on my bent legs. Unlike me, he wasn't quite finished crying. When I heard his sobs start, I tried to soothe him by stroking his short, blond hair. He turned to me and held my legs like a lifeline.

"I have no one now," he sobbed into my legs and I felt his tears running down my bare legs. I changed positions so I could pull him into a real embrace. Before I could get him all the way to me, he saw the blood stains on my dress. "Is this from when Stephan bit you?"

Shrugging, I said, "Yes. I didn't feel like going to my room to change before coming here. I didn't want to risk running into anyone. I am not feeling up to talking to anyone but you."

He let me pull him the rest of the way and laid his cheek on my shoulder. "You were kissing him." It was a statement, not a question. Never before had I known Peter to be so vulnerable, yet there he was, cuddling me and holding on to me like I was his everything.

All I did was nod to that, then lay my cheek on top of his hair. What could I say? That I fell in love with my childhood friend and

168

essentially let him die in my arms? That I never stopped loving Peter even though I loved Stephan enough to kiss him? That I was the fickle woman I had always striven not to be?

"You loved him." Another statement. "I understand."

"That makes one of us."

He lifted his head and looked into my eyes. I went on, "Before he started losing his mind, I was still confused. I know I loved him as I love you. I can't understand how I could have only today fully realized it or how it was even possible for me to feel so strongly for both of you. It seems cruel that I lost him in the same day that I realized my feelings." I paused and tilted my head, placing both my hands on Peter's face. "You are not alone, Peter. You still have me. I am so sorry I wasn't there for you today. I *did* think of you and what was happening with you."

"Stephan needed you more. You're here for me now. That's what matters." He took my hands off his face and wrapped them around his back and he lay his cheek on my shoulder again and nuzzled against my neck.

"How can you be so magnanimous with me? I broke up with you this morning." I vocalized my thoughts to him.

"Technically, *I* broke up with *you*. And I can forgive you because I am still in love with you, even after hearing you say you loved Stephan."

"I'm sorry I never told you I loved you, too. I regret that. I *do* love you."

He looked down at the blood again and traced the line, like he was remembering how that happened. I couldn't even think about how disgusting it was that he was touching my blood. "Letting you go was the hardest thing I have done in my life."

169

"We don't need to talk about this right now. I just want to be here for you now."

Placing a hand on my cheek, he said, "Always so thoughtful." He gave me a short kiss. "You're probably right. We'll talk about it later."

Peter leaned against me on my shoulder and held my hand. Aside from him ending our relationship earlier in the day, this was a side of him I had never seen before. He had never been one to really take anything seriously, but that day, he had been so sincere.

Perhaps our love is more than passionate.

I felt guilty still being in love with Peter when Stephan just died in front of my eyes.

What kind of person targets entire families regardless of age with a disease so terrible?

The way Stephan died was horrific. His wide, rapidly moving eyes, veins bulging because of his fear and screaming, and his struggling against the straps that held him down; he didn't deserve that. He deserved a long life. He deserved to participate and possibly win in the King's Test; to have a child and grow old with me.

Whoever has done this is going to pay.

My thoughts were interrupted by Peter's snoring. Until he fell asleep in Doctor Bartholomew's tutoring session, I didn't know he snored when he slept. Yawning, I decided we would just stay in the rose maze for the rest of the night.

Rotting roots to what anyone thinks. He and I both need company tonight. We've been through too much to be alone.

170

I managed to rearrange us so we were laying down on the swing and he complied, moving around in his sleep. He laid down behind me and wrapped his arm around me like I was a big teddy bear he needed to feel secure.

Just as I was about to go to sleep, I saw a figure make his way into the center of the maze. When he stepped into the moonlight, I saw it was Father. My eyes widened in fear of what he was going to do. He had a blanket in one arm, but held out his hand in a manner to let me know I didn't need to worry.

Father walked over and knelt in front of me, tears in his eyes. He looked up to try to stop the tears, but it didn't work; just as my heart was broken, his was broken for me. Kissing me on the forehead, he placed a comforting hand on my arm. Though I thought I was done crying, more tears began spilling from eyes. He took a corner of the blanket and dried them from my face.

Standing up, he unfolded the blanket and laid it over us. There was no concern on his face for me being alone with Peter. He must have known we were both grieving and needed to be with someone. After petting my hair for a moment, he turned and left.

Shortly after he left, my tears ceased and my thoughts calmed. One would think Peter's snoring would have kept me awake, but it was more soothing than the sound of rain on the roof. After pulling the blanket up so it was under my chin with one hand, I put the same hand over Peter's cuddling arms and fell asleep.

Chapter 21

When I woke up the next day, the sun was high in the air and the rose maze was warm in its rays. I removed my hands from Peter's arms and snuggled the blanket back up to my chin. When I shifted, Peter's arm gave me a squeeze.

"I was wondering when you would wake up," he said teasingly.

Yawning, I asked, "What time is it?"

Peter laughed. "I don't know. Probably sometime in the early afternoon, though."

I yawned again and moved my hand back on his arm. "I can't believe I slept that long. How long have you been awake?"

"Oh – probably a good two hours." He cuddled me closer.

"You could have woken me up, Peter."

"I didn't want to. You needed the rest and I missed having you in my arms."

I chuckled. "It's only been a day."

"Too long." He laughed and kissed my hair. I can't really explain it. It was like the day before hadn't happened – at least for the moment.

"Father came in here soon after we laid down with the blanket."

"I know. He came in while you were still sleeping and we had a quiet conversation."

Turning my head over my shoulder so I could see him, I asked, "What did you talk about?"

Peter shrugged. "He offered his condolences about my family and I forgave him for not letting me leave. We discussed your broken heart and our broken relationship. And – "

"Wait. What?"

He smirked at me. "Your father figured it out. Apparently, you mentioned me during a conversation about the King's Test the other day."

"He told you that?!" Bringing my hands to my face and turning forward again, I said, "I'm so embarrassed."

Peter squeezed me and kissed my hair again. "Don't be. I think it's sweet. Anyway. We talked about this odd and deadly disease targeting the Noble families. He's very concerned."

Putting my arms back on his, I said, "I am, too. Aside from the terror of it all, those provinces no longer have a Noble to represent them at the Council or to help keep peace in their homes." Sitting up, I stretched my arms over my head and rolled my neck to get the kinks out. Peter propped his head up on his hand and looked at me.

Feeling his gaze, I looked at him. "What?"

"I could get used to this."

"Get used to what?"

He took my hand and kissed it. "Waking up next to you. You're even beautiful with bed head."

"Gee, thanks, Peter."

"Seriously. Your morning breath isn't even that bad."

I rolled my eyes and looked down at my lap. "It's not that I'm opposed to getting back together with you or even the thought of waking up in your arms." I met his gaze again. "I feel like – I don't even know how to put it."

Guilty. Hideous. Tired. Unsure.

"I do. You only discovered your love for Stephan yesterday and now, less than a day after he died, you're realizing your love for me is stronger than you thought and you don't know what to do with it."

My mouth dropped open in shock. "Where did *this* Peter come from?"

He laughed. "What do you mean?"

"We've been together for five years and you only told me you love me a couple days ago. You have been thoughtful and serious and sincere. Far beyond simply charming and handsome." Peter smiled. "I always thought you were just having fun with me because I was a pretty girl. It never occurred to me that you actually shared the feelings I was too afraid to have or admit. Now, here you are reading my mind and comforting me in the death of another man."

Sitting up, he traced the side of my face. "I love you, Rose. I will always love you. No matter what." With a chuckle, he

175

continued. "However, I will admit that when we started a relationship, it was all about how gorgeous you were. I still remember the moment I realized it was so much more for me.

"It was about four years ago at your Birthday Ball. I was talking with Brian and Stephan when you walked in. You wore an ivory dress and had little roses of the same color woven into your hair. Even though Stephan was in the middle of talking to me, I walked over to you and kissed your hand." He kissed my hand.

"In my mind's eye, the ivory turned into a bright white and I could see you as my bride. I recognized my desire to be with you forever and it both terrified and excited me."

"I think I remember that dress and hairstyle. After kissing my hand, you made a crack about my Rose of Petrichoria title and the roses in my hair."

"I always hide things behind humor."

I nodded with a smile. "I'm starting to see that." Straightening my face, I asked, "Am I a terrible person, Peter? That I feel like nothing is broken between us, but I was only with Stephan yesterday?"

"I don't think it's even possible for you to be terrible. This is what I think: I think you were right in breaking things off – "

"*You* broke things off."

He waved his hand dismissively. "Doesn't matter. – I think if Stephan *didn't* die yesterday, you would still be struggling with your emotions. Do you know why I broke things off?"

"You admit it!"

He laughed and shook his head. "I did it because I knew you were struggling and I didn't want to get in the way of you figuring things out. I was confident that in the end, you would choose me when I had the chance to compete with him over your heart."

I giggled.

What's with all the giggling?

"You make it sound like I'm a prize to be won."

"No. You're so much more. You are the woman who stole two men's hearts without knowing it or knowing what to do with them when you finally figured it out."

I looked down and Peter swiftly turned my face to look back at him. "You would have come back to me. I know it and I think you know it. You're just so rotting roots thoughtful about others that you can't see it."

There was a silence between and he removed his hand from my face so I could look down again. Closing my eyes, I thought really hard about everything he had just said.

Is that how it would have gone? Would I really have chosen Peter between him and Stephan? Peter *certainly thinks so and thought so even before everything happened yesterday. I probably would have. I've been friends with Stephan for so long, but I've been with Peter for a long time, too.*

I looked back into Peter's brown eyes.

My time with Stephan was filled with sadness because of an evil person. Our love didn't have a chance to blossom. But my love for Peter has had five years to sow and grow. Yes. I would have chosen Peter if I really had a choice.

177

As if he was reading my mind, he leaned towards me and kissed me briefly, yet fervently. When he pressed his forehead into mine, I saw his eyes widen at my bloody dress. I looked down as well; I hadn't realized how much blood actually got on me.

"I guess I should probably go bathe and change." I said, stating the obvious.

Peter laughed. "I should, too." He began to stand and I stopped him by taking his hand. Turning back to me, he questioned what I was doing with his eyes.

"I choose you, Peter. And I don't care who knows it." He smiled and squeezed my hand before standing and leaving.

As I was walking down the glass hall back to the Core, a Guard caught up with me and trailed behind me. On my way up the stairs, I crossed paths with Father.

"Rose, I was just going to find you. I would like to speak with you," he said, all business.

Gee. I wonder what he could possibly want to talk about.

"Would you mind if I bathed and changed first? I feel like I pulled myself out of a blackberry bush," I replied.

Father looked me up and down as if only just then realizing how much of a wreck I was. As Peter had said, I had some crazy bed head. Then, there was the blood stain on my dress. I was sure I probably smelled, too.

"Alright – Come on down to my office when you have taken care of that."

"Yes, sir."

Painfully, I climbed the rest of the stairs. Though I had slept for a long time, I was still exhausted and felt like a troll was sitting on my spine. Without any grace, I slammed the button to slide open my door and wordlessly stumbled in and through to the bathroom.

"Your Highness – " Marie tried to get my attention, but I ignored her; it wasn't normal behavior for me, but I wanted to be alone for a while. I peeled off my dress and undergarments, then started the hot water. It was so rare that I ran my own bath, I didn't know where the rose oil was kept.

Hearing the bathroom door open just a bit, I looked at it and saw Marie's waving hand holding the precious scent. "Thank you, Marie."

"You are welcome, Princess."

I poured some of the oil in my bathwater and the aroma of rose filled the air. Sometimes, I felt a bit like a cliché. Though I didn't like the Rose of Petrichoria title, I *did* like roses; from their delicate scent to their soft petals – even the prick of the thorn. After turning off the water, I lowered myself into the full tub. Rather than allowing myself to fully relax right away, I washed away the tears and turmoil from the night before.

Because Father wanted to see me, I didn't have a lot of time to unwind, but I did take a few minutes to breathe in the floral scent filling the air and breathe out the sense of loss I couldn't help but feel. Stepping out of the tub, I wrapped myself up in a red towel and went back into my bedroom.

Thankfully, Marie wasn't in there; she must have taken a hint. She had always been perceptive to my needs. On my bed lay brown trousers and an ivory cowl neck tank top.

No corset today. Thank you, Marie.

To ready myself for my meeting with Father, I quickly put the clothes on, put on mascara and lip gloss, and braided my hair.

Though I knew I needed to get to Father, I sauntered down the five flights of spiral stairs so I could compose myself.

It can't go as badly as I think it will, can it? He can't be too angry about Stephan – or Peter. Or maybe he's mad because he thinks I'm being fickle with my heart. Maybe he doesn't mind that I'm in love – even though it's against the rules. Who am I kidding? Of course he's angry.

Without knocking, when I pressed the button, the door to his office slid open and I walked in. Very unlike him, he was leaning back in his chair and looking at me as if he had spent the entire time I was gone watching the door.

"Please have a seat, Rose."

No full name. A good sign?

He gestured to the chair on the opposite side of his desk – a seat I always dreaded because it only meant one thing when I was a child; I was in trouble. There had been a few times when it didn't, but, for the most part, a lecture would be about to happen.

After I did what I was told, he leaned his arms on his desk and continued. "How are you doing after yesterday?"

He's softening me…

Clearing my throat, I responded, "Alright, given the circumstances."

"I am a bit confused about something I would like for you to please clear up."

180

Here it comes…

"Yes, sir."

"Yesterday, you told me to quarantine you because you had been kissing Stephan, yes?"

I nodded.

"Then last night, I went to your swing only expecting to see you, but found you in Peter's arms."

It wasn't a question, but he paused anyway before proceeding with the lecture. I could definitely see where he was going. He wasn't angry, but he was concerned about how blasé I was being with my heart.

Father continued. "You are of course aware that it is against the rules to be in a romantic relationship before the King's Test, right?"

"Yes, sir."

He leaned back again and ran his hands down his face. "I am trying to be gentle about this since the subject is probably a tender one right now, but I really need to know what you were thinking being in a relationship at all, much less with two men."

"Weren't you and Mother in love before the Queen's Test?" I asked exasperatingly.

"Yes," he drawled. "But we were *not* in a relationship. We did *not* kiss and have secret rendezvous. And I was *not* seeing two women." He hesitated for a moment. "You haven't – uh – you know – have you?"

"Father! No!"

"I had to ask. I just wanted to be sure."

"Well, I have not done – that – with anyone! Really!" I sighed. Wringing my hands, I looked down. There was no way around it; I was going to have to tell him everything. After taking a deep breath, I explained everything. "About five years ago, I danced with Peter for the first time and we just – felt this – *pull* to each other. A couple months later, we began secreting away together. It was all laughing and fun and even though I knew it was wrong, especially because I was keeping it from you and Mother, we stayed together because we are in love."

I met his eyes. "A couple days ago, Stephan commed and said he has – had been in love with me for ten years. I was confused and Peter saw it. The morning Stephan came in, Peter broke things off. He told me today that he let me go so that I could fairly decide between them and he was sure I would choose him."

"It doesn't matter who you would have chosen. Ultimately, the King's Test will decide," Father said coldly.

This is not *going well.*

"Yes, of course. A situation that I had discussed with both of them. Peter thought he would be losing, so he just wanted to be together as much as possible over the next few weeks." I swallowed hard. "Stephan was sure he *would* win and wanted to begin our lives together now rather than later."

"Hmm."

I wasn't sure what that meant.

"Talk to me about yesterday," he commanded quietly.

"Before Stephan and I could really explore our feelings, he began exhibiting symptoms. Right after a kiss, his eyes glazed and he dropped me." I looked down. "You know the rest of what happened with him."

"Yes. Doctor Winston told me you stayed with him until the end and that his last living nightmare was something about your safety," Father said with consolation.

I rotated my eyes upwards to stop the tears before they came and failed spectacularly. Still not able to look Father in the eye, I looked back down and let tears fall. "Even though I wanted to be alone, I wasn't alone for long before Peter joined me."

Then, I met his gaze; he was beginning to cry, too. "I swear nothing happened between us last night. He and I needed each other even if I didn't know it at first. I couldn't cry anymore, but he sobbed and sobbed, and I pet his head, like Mother does for me when I'm sad, and tried to coo him into some kind of solace. It just couldn't be done. He was so upset about his family. I couldn't send him away."

I huffed. "I didn't want to go back to my room and Peter didn't want to be alone, so we laid down and I let him hold me because he needed it.

"I never stopped loving Peter. I know I loved Stephan, but I don't know to what degree because we never got to figure it out. Honestly, I must tell you that Peter and I patched things up this morning and I have no intention of ending our relationship until after my Birthday Ball." I pressed my quivering lips into a straight line and jutted my chin to let him know I meant business.

Father sniffled and relaxed a little; just a little. "I'm not very happy about this, Miriam."

Ooo. He used my real name. This is serious.

After pursing his lips and biting his cheek while deep in thought, he nodded as if he made a decision. "While I am *not* happy about this *at all*, I am going to let it fly and stay flying until your Birthday Ball." He leaned forward. "I am only allowing it because of how difficult yesterday was for both of you. You're right. Neither of you should be alone."

"Thank you, Father. Please forgive me for breaking the rule to begin with."

"I forgive you." He exhaled loudly. "Now that *that's* taken care of, I want to request your presence at a Council meeting in the morning concerning this mutated Daze. Doctor Winston will be there and without me mentioning you, he suggested your attendance as well."

I quirked a brow. "He did?"

"Apparently, he was impressed with you yesterday."

"Huh. Well, I'll be there. What time?"

"8:00."

I took a deep breath, sniffled, and stretched my arms over my head. "What time is it right now?"

He looked at the clock on his holocomm device. "5:00."

"If it's alright with you, I think I'll skip dinner tonight. I need to try to get my mind straight again after the last few days."

"That's alright with me. I'll let your mother know."

We both stood up at the same time and Father rounded his desk quickly to embrace me. I pulled us apart and he squeezed my arms one more time before I went straight back up the Core and to my room; I didn't run into anybody and I didn't seek anyone out. Marie was sitting on my sofa and was surprised to see me back so soon, but didn't hesitate to help me get ready when I said I just wanted to go to bed because I had an early morning coming up.

~ ~ ~

Five coffins sit on a platform. Four are wooden. One is glass and I'm lying in it. The silhouette of man the color of the night sky circles the row of coffins and lays a hand on the wooden one on the end. It disappears.

I slowly opened an eye to squint at the clock when I heard someone knocking at the door. The only light available was a slit of dim green from the Space Needle coming between the curtains of my window, but it was enough to make my head feel like it was going to explode.

Who is visiting me at 3:00 in the morning?

"Rose?"

I closed my eye again.

Peter. Maybe if I don't answer, he'll go away. I can't do anymore talking tonight.

He knocked again and I did not respond again. At that point, I heard a murmured conversation begin between Peter and the Guard at my door.

"My Lord, if she is not responding, I must insist you take your leave. The Princess has been through quite a lot lately," said my Guard.

"I understand that. That's why I am here. I am here to check in on her. She has not left her room all afternoon and evening."

"She has been resting, Duke Peter."

There was an awkward silence. It must have been the first time Peter had been addressed by his new title. Squeezing my eyes tight again, I sighed and pulled myself out of bed. The conversation outside my room continued, though I was no longer paying close enough attention to understand anything. After throwing on a robe, I opened the door and lazily leaned into the doorway. I still only had one eye open and I could feel my braid had come undone in several places. Peter smirked at my dishevelment and I could tell he was remembering my bedhead from earlier in the day.

"Isalright," I slurred to the Guard. "Comeonin, Peter."

The Guard nodded as he stepped aside and I gently pulled Peter in by his hand. Because my back was to him, I wasn't positive, but I was pretty sure Peter gave the Guard a dirty look on his way in. When the door closed, I dropped Peter's hand, shuffled over to my small sofa, and plopped myself into the plush seat.

As I squinted open my other eye, I patted the seat next to me so he would sit. He chuckled as he sat. "You look horrible."

"Gee, thanks, Peter." I rubbed my eyes with the heels of my hands and yawned, "What is it that you need?"

"Why is it so dark in here? Why don't you have any lights on?"

Then *I* gave him a dirty look. "Why do *you* suppose, darling?"

"Darling?" he asked me, clearly amused.

I waved a frustrated hand at him. "The lights are off because I was *asleep*. It is 3:00 AM, Peter! The better question is 'what are you doing in my room at 3:00 AM?'"

Leaning against the back of the sofa, he pulled me over to him so my head was on his shoulder. "Fair enough. I was worried when I didn't see or hear from you all day. I couldn't sleep without knowing if you were alright."

186

Snuggling in, I murmured, "I'm alright. I just have an early morning and haven't had much sleep – "

I woke up to Peter gently shaking me. "Oh. Sorry. What was I saying?"

He chuffed. "That you haven't had much sleep and you have an early morning. Me, too."

"Right – Council meeting."

I barely woke to my blankets being pulled up to my chin and Peter kissing my forehead. "Good night, *darling.*" Peter said.

"Shut up, Peter. Love you."

Chapter 22

When I strode into the Council Chambers, everyone in the room stood because of my rank; Father followed closely behind and we all sat after he did. Looking around, I was acutely aware of the three empty seats dispersed throughout the table; Peter now sat in the seat for the Juniper Noble household. The elected Delegates for Cedar, Willow, Oak, and Juniper Provinces had the same signs of weeping that Peter and I both had, which wasn't surprising. In our system of government, the Nobles and Delegates worked closely together and because of that, their families were often good friends.

Despite what Father had said the previous day, Darrel wasn't there; I figured he must still be figuring things out. The Dukes and Duchesses around the table were understandably shifting nervously; they were probably wishing they were at home with their families right now. To me, they seemed beyond uncomfortable or homesick, though. Puffy eyes indicated they had been crying or afraid the night before, and I tried not to notice the Duchess of Birch rubbing her temples like she had a headache.

Standing, Father addressed the Council. "Nobles and Delegates, I thank you for coming to this emergency meeting of the Arborian Council. As you are all aware, we have recently lost all of three Noble families and all but one of another." He nodded somberly to Peter. "I know this sudden tragedy has hit us hard in a variety of ways, but it is important to try to set aside our emotions so we can look ahead and decide on the next steps."

Delegate Maple was the first to speak. "Clearly, Your Majesty, new Nobility will need to be appointed for the Cedar, Willow, and Oak Provinces." Because of the current circumstances, I had been hoping he would tone it down, but Delegate Maple brought out his fabulous color of condescension anyway. I always felt bad that my uncle had to work with him. "The Council cannot operate like this for long. I have taken the initiative to make a list of promising families I would like to pass around the table."

Everyone jumped in their seats when Delegate Oak slapped his hands flat on the table. "Delegate Maple, the Noble families are hardly cold and you have already made a list?! This is completely inappropriate!"

Delegate Maple gave Delegate Oak a level glare. "While I understand you are going through quite a lot, Oak, the continuing function of the government needs to take some form of precedence in our discussion today."

Delegate Oak's face was completely red, the tips of his ears were even red, from his anger. "I agree that the issue needs to be discussed today, but not immediately. Surely, we should discuss honoring and burying those who have passed within the last several days first."

"I concur with Oak," The Duchess of Birch said, now simply poking her index finger next to her eyebrow. "I move to table the discussion of selecting new Nobility until the end of this Council session."

"Seconded," Delegate Oak unsurprisingly said.

"All in favor?" Father asked.

All but Delegate Maple "ayed."

"All against?"

Delegate Maple "nayed."

"Movement accepted. Now, let us discuss the honoring of the Noble families."

The Delegates from the nobleless provinces and Delegate Juniper were put together as a committee to plan the memorial services and that was about all that was said concerning our dead friends.

The conversation quickly shifted to bureaucratic discussions about paperwork, finances, law, and other things that probably should have concerned me, but didn't. I glanced over to The Duchess of Birch, who was now sweating through her lovely sea foam green blouse; she really wasn't doing well. I was concerned for her and, as an extension, for Brian.

Then, I looked over to Peter, who was dutifully paying attention, but I could tell he was about as interested in the volume of this year's sap harvest as I was. Honestly, I was wondering why we were even discussing it at the meeting. It was supposed to be an urgent session about the mutated Daze.

Next thing I knew, I found myself infuriated with the people surrounding me. Could they seriously only see the superficial bandages that needed to be applied? What about the other families? What about poor The Duchess of Birch who was obviously unwell?

"I think we need to discuss the King's Test, Majesty," Delegate Juniper pulled me out of my thoughts of enrage. Peter was also shaken from his thoughts and gave his province's Delegate an incredulous look.

"What of it?" I found myself unintentionally asking out loud.

Delegate Juniper and Peter both looked at me. "Two of the seven participants have died, Your Highness. Surely, the Test will need to be reorganized. Possibly even rewritten." She looked to Father. "Only you know what the King's Test consists of, Your Majesty. Is this something we should be concerned about or will it be able to take place as scheduled?"

My mouth dropped. "A bit eager to see Duke Peter crowned, Juniper?" Delegate Maple belligerently asked. Peter was then even more aghast than he had already been. My mouth dropped further. To his credit, Duke Maple, my uncle, was shaking his head with embarrassment.

Before things could get any uglier, Father spoke, "I will have to do some shifting and rewriting, and the Test will likely be two months rather than three, but we should be able to start on schedule."

Slowly standing, I smoothed my hands over the round, wooden conference table and addressed the men and women present. Simply standing up garnered their attention. "Gentlemen, Ladies. I think we are forgetting something very important here; far more important than paperwork and suitors."

All eyes were still on me, then, including those of Father. "Three of ten Noble families are completely wiped out. One is down to only a Duke." I couldn't meet Peter's eyes. "I think it is imperative that we put extra Guards on the remaining Noble households."

The Duchess of Birch spoke up. "I must say that I agree with the Princess. Brian has put on a brave face, but Brianna is afraid." She was talking about Count Brian and his twin sister.

Delegate Alder responded. "I understand the fear that must be present among the Nobility, but I fail to see what more Guards will

192

accomplish. The Cedars, Willows, Junipers, and Oaks all died from a disease, yes?"

"Yes, they did, Delegate Alder," I said. "But Doctor Winston has a current hypothesis that the Noble families are being targeted. Perhaps stationing more Guards will keep out suspicious individuals that may make it passed the few that are already stationed there."

"A hypothesis? You wish to reassign the Royal Arborian Guard over a hypothesis?" Delegate Alder asked.

"She is not wrong, Delegate Alder. I have been speaking with Doctor Winston as well and he seems to believe it to be true. It is more than a hypothesis; it is an educated hypothesis," Father defended me.

Thank you, Father. Wait. Wasn't Darrel supposed to be here?

"I sincerely doubt that every one of Doctor Winston's hypotheses have turned out to be true," Delegate Alder said with disbelief.

"Doctor Winston was going to come today, but was in the middle of a test when the meeting began," Father said.

"I move to add more security to the remaining Noble households," Peter blurted.

"Seconded," the Duchess of Birch said.

"All in favor?" asked Father

"Aye," the seven Nobles said.

"All against?" asked Father.

"Nay," said the ten Delegates.

"The 'nays' have it. We will not be adding more security to the Noble households."

When the vote went through, I was still standing. I was so furious, I began shaking. There was a dead silence in the room and no one could meet each other's eyes. Knowing that some of the Delegates only voted 'nay' because the other Delegates did made me see red. Balling my fists at my side, I calmly said, "Please excuse me. I have some important matters to take care of."

Before anyone could say anything, I walked out and marched straight to Darrel's lab. How I wished that we still had doors that I could slam. I had never done it, but I had read about it in quite a few novels and it seemed like an action that could take some of my anger out of my system.

I was mostly shocked that even the Delegates of the provinces that lost their Nobles did not vote in favor of Peter's motion. They saw with their own eyes what we were facing and they did nothing. No. They did *not* do nothing. They voted the rest of the Nobles to their deaths. They made themselves a part of the problem rather than a part of the solution.

As I walked, I briefly entertained the notion that we had a conspiracy going on.

Do the Delegates want *the rest of the Nobles dead? How could they go about making this virus without anyone finding out? No. Delegates Willow, Juniper, Cedar, and Oak genuinely looked distraught, and Delegate Maple even had a list of families to consider.*

Could it be the beginning of a revolution to overthrow the Crown? Surely Father would have informed me if there was any growing unrest among the people. I personally haven't heard anything directly.

When I made it to Darrel's lab, I walked in without knocking and made my way to the opposite side of the table where he sat. He was hunched over the Duke of Juniper, Peter's father, examining his brain. I could have gone the rest of my life without seeing his head cut in half with his brain exposed being poked at with some pointy metal medical instrument.

"Good morning, Miriam," Darrel said without looking up.

Trying not to vomit, I said, "It is actually afternoon now, Darrel. It is a little after 1:00. Have you eaten anything today?"

He looked over his glasses at me and replied, "Would you feel hungry right now if you were doing what I am doing?"

"Touché."

"How is it that I can help you, Miriam?"

Still somehow remaining calm, I said, "I was wondering how your research was coming along. Have you made it to a point where you can definitively say the Nobles are being targeted?"

He straightened himself, then arched his back in a stretch. "I could use a break. Let us have a seat."

As we walked to his office, I considered the gruesome experiments his job had recently began requiring. I couldn't imagine doing such things as cutting the head of someone I knew in half or slicing them open to examine their insides. Granted, Darrel wasn't particularly *close* with any of the Nobility, but he had rubbed elbows with them at the various special occasions at the palace.

Rather than going to his desk, he threw a blanket and pillow off the plush sofa and plopped himself down upon it. I lowered myself gently onto the sofa; princesses do *not* plop in public.

195

"Have you been sleeping in your office?" I asked.

Darrel rubbed his eyes with his fingers and yawned. "Yes. I have only slept a little since the bodies got here. No point in going back to my house when I am only going to be getting a half hour of sleep at any given time."

"Oh, Darrel," I sympathized. "Thank you for your dedication to this. All the Noble families are afraid and it will do them good to hear that you are working around the clock on this situation."

"It is what I do," he groaned. After a pause, he said, "About your question. Yes. I have determined that the Noble families whose bodies have come here were targeted."

"I figured as much. Are you working on a cure?"

Darrel sighed. "I am trying to figure out a way to do it. The problem is that each virus is different. It makes it difficult to create a cure for everyone. I will probably have to assess each reported instance on a case by case basis."

"I thought it was a mutated version of the Daze. Can you not make a cure based on the original Daze?"

"It is certainly a place to start, but the problem lies in the way the virus was created. Whoever created these viruses knew what he was doing; he is brilliant. It appears that whoever engineered *this* variant used multiple sets of viruses as the delivery systems. Meaning he created viruses that cannot spread on their own and generally do not replicate and die, unless someone has *also* been infected with another virus. Without knowing each set of matched pairs of viruses, it makes it really hard to predict.

"The fact that the families have died synchronously is some kind of a crazy coincidence. There is no way he could have made it to have a specific time it would be released."

"I do not understand. I thought the Daze was killing them."

"There are no suicides among those who have died. If the Daze was progressed to the point of bringing death upon its host, statistically we would have had a few suicides. No. Each family has died from whatever affliction was raging their system.

"For example, Stephan died of a heart attack. He was a perfectly healthy and strong young man, but the Oak's Daze activated arrhythmogenic right ventricular dysplasia, a rare genetic heart condition where normal heart tissue progressively transforms into fat and scar tissue. Our genius scientist must have figured a way to increase the rate of growth and that, in turn, brought each member of the family into cardiac arrest.

"It was a condition that was fixed genetically in people who had it decades ago. After the fix, it was no longer passed on as a disease, but as an immunity, so no one in the Oak family has had it since then.

"In order to begin developing cures for the remaining households, I will need to take blood samples from each family."

"That is assuming they are already afflicted."

"Right. Another reason for me to collect blood would be to determine if they are."

I shrugged. "That should not be a problem. The Nobles are all here for a special meeting of the Council. I will be heading back to the meeting after this and I will let them know that they need to stop by here before leaving. I have what I need from you, so I will let you get back to your work. Should they require a statement from you, would I be able to comm you?"

"Yes, of course. I will just rest in here for a while so I can be near a holocomm in case you need me." He closed his eyes sleepily.

Standing up, I said, "Thank you, again, Darrel. For everything."

He gave me a sharp nod and I turned to leave. Rather than walk like I did on my way to the lab, I jogged back towards the Council Chamber. Anticipation and anxiety shot through me and gave me a jolt of adrenaline. I was ready to face the room of pretentious Delegates and give them a generous slice of humble pie.

As soon as I made it inside the palace, I knew something was awry. I picked up my speed and ran into the open door of the Council Chamber. Chaos had taken the reigns of the meeting. Looking around, everyone's body language displayed their emotions like a flame on a dark night. Some people were crying. Some were angry. Some were in shock. Everyone had some negative emotion ruling their mind. When I made it to the table, I saw what everyone was upset about. The Duchess of Birch was lying dead on the floor.

Bringing my hand to my mouth to squelch a cry of angst, I slowly took my seat at the table. A moment later, two men came in with a hover stretcher and removed her body from the Chamber, I guessed to bring her to Darrel.

After they left, Father said, "Everyone please return to your seats. We have much to discuss."

Everyone made their way to their chairs; Delegate Birch didn't look like he was in any state to vote on anything. The ogre of a man frowned at the table like it was the cause of the Duchess' death.

"I move to add more security to the Noble households," he said mildly after there was silence for a time.

"Seconded," said Delegate Alder.

"All in favor?" asked Father.

"Aye," said everyone.

198

"All against?"

No one said anything.

"Very well. I will get together with the High General after this meeting and get more Guards out there." He looked over to me. "Princess Miriam, I am guessing you left to have a conversation with Doctor Winston about the Daze?"

"Yes, sir."

"What did he say?"

"He has determined that the Noble families are being targeted. Unfortunately, each family has a slightly different mutation of the Daze, so an overall cure is likely not possible. He will need to develop a cure for each of the remaining families."

"But – we do not know that each remaining family has the disease," said the Duchess of Sequoia with a fearful tremble in her low voice.

"That is true," I replied. "That is why Doctor Winston needs to take a blood sample from each of you here. He will be able to determine if you have the virus and, if you do, he can begin working on a cure. I would recommend you do that quickly and return home to your families."

"I have concerns for the Royal family," said Delegate Maple. Because he had only ever shown disdain for Father and me, his statement surprised me. "I think Evergreen Palace should be put on lock-down until all of this is taken care of. No one should come in or out after the Council leaves."

"I agree. So moved," said the Duke of Maple, Father's brother.

"Seconded," said Delegate Birch.

"All in favor?" Father asked.

Everyone voted, "Aye."

"The ayes have it. After the Council departs, there will be a quarantine put on Evergreen Palace. No one will enter or leave the grounds."

Chapter 23

Everyone left the Council Chamber shortly after voting in the quarantine. Before Father left, he told me to join him at 4:00 PM for his meeting with High General Francis Miller.

Peter and I walked together out the door and onto the royal trail through the forest so we could have some semblance of privacy. Even though my Guard was behind us a ways, it was nice to get outside and wander a bit. To try to forget for just a moment the evil lurking somewhere in the shadows. For a while, we walked together with only the sound of birds tweeting and our feet crunching through the dirt as our soundtrack.

"I wonder if the rest of the Birches are gone," Peter said.

I shrugged and sighed. "Probably, if it follows suit with the other four houses. Poor Brian. He showed such promise."

"He seemed like kind of a tool on the dance floor."

I smiled and shook my head. "He made up for it in the interview. He was so intimidated and awed by me, he actually cried after he kissed me."

"Huh."

After another pause, Peter asked, "Why do you think it is that I was not infected with the virus, but the rest of my family was?"

Bringing my eyebrows together, I considered this. "Perhaps you were here when the infection was introduced. You and Ella do spend more time here than any other Nobles. There is no way of knowing how long it was in your family's systems. There is also the possibility you were somehow purposefully missed."

Peter breathed out a shaky breath. "I'm going to miss them. I already do. I don't feel ready to be the Duke, yet. I don't – "

I turned and put my fingers on his lips to interrupt him. "Peter, worry will not help you. I know you feel very alone right now with your family gone, but you must know that Father will be available for you if you have any questions about your duties as Duke. I'm sure Uncle Edmond will help, too. And you have me for all the emotional support you need."

After bringing my hand down, I stood on my tip toes and gave him a peck. He smiled. "I know. Thank you for being there for me, Rose."

"Miriam! Peter!" I looked around to find the source of our shouted names. The voice was familiar; it was Ella. She only ever used my real name when she was angry about something.

"Ella?" I shouted in return.

She finally caught up with us and bent over with her hands on her knees, huffing and puffing like she just ran a marathon. "Is everything alright, Ella?"

"No! Everything is *not* alright! How could you let them impose a quarantine, Miriam? How am I supposed to get to my family if anything happens?"

"I assumed your father would bring you home with him. He didn't appear to have any symptoms, though, Ella."

"Healthy as a bear," Peter agreed.

"That's beside the point," said Ella. "*If* anything happens, I'm stuck here! No offense, but if I'm going to die, I don't want to die here."

"You're not going to die, Ella. I won't let that happen," I said.

"And how are you going to stop it? This virus has now taken out half the Noble houses."

"Yes, but now we know what is going on. It's not like I made the decision unilaterally. It's a necessary precaution the Council agreed upon." I didn't feel it prudent to tell her it was a unanimous vote. "Tell you what," I continued "I'll go down to Darrel's lab and ask that he check the Maple blood first. If your family has the virus, I'll see to it that he works on your cure first."

"Who's Darrel?"

"Doctor Winston."

"Since when are you on a first name basis with Doctor Winston?"

"Does it really matter?" I asked, throwing my hands up in exasperation.

"I don't particularly like it, myself, Rose," Peter piped in, crossing his arms over his chest.

I looked between the two of them. Ella was smirking and Peter looked even angrier than he already was. "Oh, come on! He's a *friend.* We've mingled enough with him that it's kind of weird we *haven't* been on a first name basis already."

"The King doesn't even call him Darrel, Miriam," said Ella, still using my real name.

"We're getting off track here. It doesn't matter what I call Darrel – Doctor Winston – whatever! I want to know if that idea sounds satisfactory for you, Ella."

"Yeah. Since you're going by first names now, I don't doubt you can make it happen."

"I'm sure," added Peter.

"Jealous, much?" I asked him.

"Jealous? What do I have to be jealous of? He's a big dweeb. And I'm handsome and charming. You've even said so yourself. I'm sure Ella agrees." He waggled his eyebrows at her and we all started laughing. I was glad for the levity he brought into the conversation. He had a way of making me laugh even in dire circumstances.

"Alright, then. I'll head on over and talk with him. Ella, you come with me and let him take a blood sample. Just to make sure you're safe," I said.

"I'm coming, too. I would like to be there when you speak with *Darrel,*" Peter said.

"I'm sure I'm fine. Like Peter said, no one in my family is showing any symptoms," Ella said. Though, she was probably more reassuring herself than Peter and me.

Placing my hand on her shoulder and meeting her eyes with mine, I said, "I know. But *I* would feel better knowing you're safe. Can you do it for me?"

Giving me a hug and with a sigh, she said, "Yeah. I'll do it for you."

"Maybe we can switch *Darrel's* focus over to Ella while we're down there," Peter teased.

I slapped his arm with the back of my hand and laughed. The three of us made our way back to the palace and to Darrel's lab. Upon entering, Darrel loudly said, "Come on back to my office, Miriam." I grimaced at the use of my name.

Peter quirked his brow at me and I shrugged helplessly. I hadn't mentioned that Darrel was calling me by my first name, too. Apparently, Peter disapproved.

We all walked into Darrel's office and he sat up straighter in his desk chair when we all entered the room. "Oh. I did not know you brought others, Mir – Princess Miriam."

Thank you for having the common sense to use my title in front of my friends.

It was too late for Peter, though. He was already glaring at Darrel with his arms folded over his chest again. Peter was obviously flexing his biceps. If they had antlers, I'm sure they would have been ramming into each other. I stifled a laugh with a mental picture of their antlers locking.

"I was wondering if you had a chance to look at the blood tests, yet," I said.

"I only have results for two of the families," Darrel replied. He tapped a few buttons on his console and opened the results for the tests. "Actually, it looks like I have three now. Sequoia, Elm, and – Maple." He said the last with hesitation and his face paled.

I inhaled sharply and glanced at Ella. Her eyes were already welling up with tears. Without even stating the results, we all knew what the results were for Maple.

Gently, and without looking up from his console, Darrel said, "I am so, so sorry. But all three have tested positive." He stood up and walked around his desk to Ella and placed his hand on her arm. "Countess Elleouise, I will immediately begin work on your family's cure. I will not rest until I have succeeded."

Ella nodded, but didn't say anything. I asked, "Doctor, do you think you could run some tests for Ella. She has not been exhibiting any symptoms, but I just want to be sure she is safe."

"Of course," Darrel said as he removed his hand from Ella. "I think it would be best if we keep her here for observation until I get results from the tests."

"I will stay with her," I said.

After a pause, Darrel said, "Um – I am on orders from the King to not allow you near anyone or anything that could be infected, Princess."

"Father ordered what?!" I asked incredulously.

Holding his hands palm out as if in surrender, Darrel said, "Do not shoot the messenger."

Ella looked at me and said, "It's ok, Rose. I'll be alright."

Pursing my lips, I gave a curt nod, turned on my heel and marched out of the lab. Peter struggled to keep up as I kept a fast pace all the way to Father's office. I noted the wide eyes and quick steps of the maids and butlers as I passed. I was mad, and it was obvious to everyone. Without knocking, I entered Father's office.

Not even giving me the curtesy of looking up from his console, Father said, "Hello, dear."

"Hello? Is that *all* you have to say to me?" I demanded. Peter shifted uncomfortably on his feet.

Glancing over his glasses, he said, "You are mad."

"Very astute, Father."

Removing his glasses and sitting up, he said, "What are you mad about, Rose?"

"Why in the world did you tell Doctor Winston to not allow me in the lab?"

"Peter, can you excuse us, please?" Father asked, then waited for him to leave. "Do you really need to ask that question? You are the *only* direct heir to the Crown. I cannot risk you getting infected with something down there."

"You know just as well as I do that there is no risk of me catching the Daze from any body in that lab, much less Ella."

"I didn't say anything about Ella."

"Well, she's getting her blood tested and Doctor Winston wouldn't let me stay with her."

Father slapped his hand on his desk and shouted, "I don't want you in that lab. That's all there is to it!"

"Roots, Father! There is no *good* reason."

"Language, young lady! You're taking on too much. You're not the Queen, yet. Roots! You are not even the Crown Princess, yet!"

Taken aback by his statement, and hypocritical use of foul speech, I quieted down. "Do you think I am not ready to be Crown Princess?"

"I didn't say that."

"It was implied. If you won't let me take on the responsibilities expected of a Crown Princess, how do you expect me to rule someday?"

Father dragged his hands down his face, then rubbed the back of his neck with one hand. Lowering his voice, he said, "I know you're ready, dear. I'm just – this whole situation has me scared out of my wits. I have no control over the solution beyond placing Guards up at the Noble houses. Please, humor me, Rose. I love you and I would never forgive myself if anything happened to you that I could have prevented."

Folding my arms and tapping my foot, I stood there silently, considering what he said. In his place, I probably would have done the same thing. Still frustrated, I relented to his will. "Very well," I said, taking a seat in the chair opposite him. "Why *did* you and Mother only have me? Why not have more children?"

"I'm surprised it took you this long to ask that question. We spent most of your early childhood dreading the day you'd ask for a brother or sister." Sighing, he said, "We did try before you and after you, but your mother miscarried both times."

"Miscarriage? But that hardly ever happens anymore."

"Right. We took it as a sign that we needed to be happy with what we had: you. We poured all our love into you and prayed daily that you would grow to become a good and wise Queen." He reached across his desk and took my hand. "I don't doubt that we succeeded. You will likely be a better ruler than even me. You have this desire to not simply rule the people, but to serve them; that is what a real leader is: a servant. Many Kings and Queens don't believe that, which is why many monarchies in history failed."

"Thank you, Father. That means a lot to me."

Removing his hand from mine, he said, "I do have some news I think you would be interested in hearing. It appears that over the last several hours, the rest of the Birch family and the Duke and Duchess of Sequoia have died."

"Over the last several hours? You mean, they didn't die at once? And the Sequoia children are still alive?"

"Yes, though I would imagine they won't be alive for long."

"Right. Poor Brian." After another moment, I said, "This may sound callous, but that will only leave four participants for the King's Test, assuming the other men survive this."

Father nodded. "I've considered that."

After chewing on my cheek for a moment, I asked, "What will we do if they all die? There will be no one left for me to marry."

"Do you think Peter will die?"

Swallowing hard, I said, "I hope not. I didn't think so before you told me about the Birches and Sequoias."

Sighing, Father said, "*If* the rest of the men die, we'd have to extend the invitation to Royalty from other countries."

"Couldn't we just wait for the new Nobility to be elected and wait for their children to come of age?"

"No. While you went to talk with Doctor Winston, and while we still haven't decided who will receive the honor, the Council decided that the new Nobility will be young adults with no children.

That way, the children will be born into Nobility and there won't be any qualms among the people about who is the right heir. We would have to wait at *least* twenty years. That is much too long. You would be past your prime for having children."

I wanted to be offended that my fertility was coming into play, but could not deny its importance. I glanced at the clock on Father's Computer Desk. "High General Miller is running late. It's 4:15."

"Yes. He is having to bring his thirteen year old son with him. He was off duty today and his wife is otherwise occupied or I wouldn't allow it. When I asked for you to join us for the meeting, it was so you could observe the meeting, but it would be more useful if you could sit with the boy and keep him occupied."

I quirked a brow. "Father, I have no clue what I would talk about with a teenage boy."

"Anything. Just don't let him interrupt his father and me."

Before I could protest further, Father's office door chimed and he allowed entrance. I gave him a look and he smirked at me in victory.

Oh. This is so *not over.*

High General Miller and his boy came in and bowed. "King Aaron. Princess Miriam." We both nodded acknowledgment of their bows and they stood at attention. I had never met the High General's son before, but he was a spitting image of his Father. The High General was slightly taller than me and his son was slightly shorter. They both had military cropped black hair and blue eyes.

Father and I were both standing and extended our hands for shakes. "High General Miller. Francis." Father greeted.

Francis? Poor kid got his dad's name.

"I do not believe I have met you, Francis, but I have been hearing great things," Father said conversationally.

Francis' eyes widened. "You have, sir?"

"Yes. You have been quite successful in the running and strength competitions at the Petrichorian Academy, yes? Have you considered joining the Royal Arborian Guard like your father? Perhaps someday you can be the High General for Princess Miriam when she becomes Queen."

Francis beamed. "Why, yes, sir. I have top marks in strength and have broken records in running for the PA. I already plan on joining the Royal Arborian Guard. I train with Father every morning before he leaves for work."

Father put a heavy hand on his shoulder. "Good lad." Father gave me a sidelong glance.

That's my cue.

"Come, sit with me, Francis. Tell me some more about your plans."

Francis' grin widened and his face turned raspberry red as he followed me over to the sofa. I rolled my eyes while he was still behind me.

Boys. Always judging me on appearance.

Sitting down, I looked to the side at a maid and asked for a couple cups of coffee and she scuttled off. I briefly considered having an IV of coffee injected so I didn't have to drink so much simply to stay awake lately. Glancing over, I saw that Father and High General Miller were already huddled over his desk figuring out the new Guard assignments.

Francis cleared his throat nervously and I looked at him. "Pardon, Princess Miriam. If you do not mind me saying so, you are lovely today. I – I have never seen you in person before." The High General heard him and made horrified eye contact with me. Father patted his arm reassuringly as if to let him know I can handle it.

Thanks a lot, Father.

Looking to the young man, I politely said, "Thank you. Tell me about your running, Francis. I did not have the privilege of schooling with other people, so I was never able to compete in anything."

"Well, I hate to brag," Francis began in a tone that said he was actually very excited to brag, "but let us just say I can run a mile in four and a half minutes."

Feigning interest, I said, "Trees and Blossoms! That *is* impressive." I honestly had no idea if it was or not, but Francis did not know that. What did it hurt to stroke his ego a bit?

"It is too bad you were never able to compete in dance, Princess. You are the best dancer I have ever seen," Francis flattered. I nonchalantly glanced over to Father who sneakily held a finger out from the edge of the table to let me know I only had to hold out a little longer.

"When have you seen me dance, Francis? Has your father brought you to a ball?"

He shrugged. "No, but my mother always watches the first few minutes just to watch you and Count Peter dance The Rose. I will admit, the closest thing to dancing I have seen or participated in aside from that are the formals at the Academy. The only dancing really done there is swaying to and fro in rhythm – sometimes. Mainly, the dancing is all about how close you can get to your dance partner." He slapped his hand over his mouth and turned red again and I laughed.

"No need to be embarrassed, Francis. I am sure that is a universal truth among all dancers. Though I have never been allowed such goals, it is certainly true even at balls, where dancing is a bit more formal than swaying to and fro."

Francis furrowed his brow. "What do you mean, Princess? That you have not been allowed such goals?"

I'm not sure why I went on, but I did. I was his age when I learned about the King's Test after all. "Well, being the heir to the Crown, I have been expressly forbidden any form of romance so that whoever wins the King's Test will have all of me and nothing else. I will not be missing pieces of my heart, nor will I bring baggage with me into my marriage."

His frown deepened. "That is hardly fair."

"No, it is not. But that is just a part of being the Princess. The more power a person has, the more he or she has to give up. Do not get me wrong. It is not that it is not a big deal, but it is something I have been aware of and preparing for since I was thirteen."

"Can the King's Test not be discontinued?"

I looked over and noticed our fathers were finished and watching us intently. Francis' father looked thoughtful and *my* father looked curious as to how this conversation would end. I briefly wondered how long they had been listening, but Francis was completely oblivious.

"No, Francis. It cannot. As much as it is a terrible sacrifice to make, it keeps things peaceful among the Nobility. Because the heir keeps her heart her own, there is no room for anyone to complain about fairness. Even if she *were* to fall in love, it would not matter because the final decision is made by the King, not the Princess."

At the mention of "the King," Francis looked over to our fathers. He didn't look embarrassed at being caught in the conversation. Standing, he gave Father a curt bow and walked out of his office without another word.

"I – I am sorry, sir. I have never seen him like that. I will certainly have a talk with him about what kind of respect he should be showing to you." High General Miller was, understandably, appalled at his son's behavior.

Father patted his arm reassuringly again. "It is not an issue, Francis. I know how teenagers are." Father gave him a wink and High General Miller sighed in relief. Bowing to each of us, he followed his son out the door.

What a strange boy.

Chapter 24

Dinner seemed so quiet without Ella there. Peter was still pretty angry for not being allowed to bury his family, so he stayed quiet through the meal. When Peter and Ella left from visiting, it always felt like there was a hole in the palace. My best friends seemed to complete me. Without Stephan, my small circle had become even smaller, but I was grateful I still had Ella and Peter. I just prayed I still would when everything was said and done.

Part way through the meal, the Steward came in to deliver the news that the rest of the Sequoias had died and that the Duke of Maple was beginning to show signs of madness. At the news, we all simultaneously lost our appetites and Father began to weep for his brother.

Mother and I embraced him and allowed him the moment of weakness. The Guards averted their eyes and the waitresses left the room without needing to be told. After a while, Ella came in. Ella had clearly been sobbing and she ran over and joined in the family embrace while Peter sat awkwardly in his chair.

Father and Mother excused themselves to go to their room. Ella and I shifted so we were still embracing; she was still crying. Suddenly, I felt two strong arms take us into a wider embrace and I extended my arm to include Peter.

"I'm so sorry about your family, Ella," Peter said. "I know what it's like."

"I know," Ella cracked.

I wanted to ask about her results, but it didn't seem like the proper time. Also, I could induce that the results were negative simply by the fact she was there. I had an irrational combination of relief, gladness, and grief because of how life had been recently and I suddenly did not want to be without my best friend and boyfriend that night.

"Why don't you both stay with me tonight? I can have the maid bring in a cot for you, Peter, and Ella, you can share my bed. I don't think any of us should be alone."

"I don't understand how or why Peter and I can be uninfected when our families *were*. It makes no sense," Ella said.

"I agree, but until we figure out who's behind everything, there is no way to know for sure. I'm assuming your families were either purposely or accidentally infected while you were both here at some point."

Peter let go of Ella and stole me out of her arms. Laying his cheek on the top of my head, he said, "Please tell me you've been tested and you're negative."

"I've been tested and I'm negative."

With that, he let go and we made our way to my room. On the way, I stopped a maid and asked that a cot be brought to my room. She nodded and rushed off to find one. While Ella and I went straight there, Peter stopped off at his room to put on something to sleep in. I simply lent a night gown to Ella for the night.

"Rose?"

"Yes, Ella?"

"I want to go to my family."

I did not answer right away. "It's not possible, Ella."

She bit her lip. "Not legally."

I narrowed my eyes. "What do you mean?"

"I know there are secret tunnels, Rose. I have been coming here my whole life and I have never asked you to show me. However, I'm sure you know where they are and I want you to show me one now. Help me leave."

"I do know where they are, but it is madness to leave, Ella. If you go home, you could very well contract the disease you do not have now and die."

"I understand that." Ella sniffled. "Please, Rose."

"Do you *really* understand? Do you know what you are asking me to do? We just lost Stephan yesterday. *Stephan!* My brother-in-heart! Peter could be out of our lives in a few months after the King's Test. You are really the only friend I have left that I know will still be around in a few months."

"And you have always been the only one I can really count on," Ella said firmly. "Please, Rose."

She was right. We had always been there for each other; even through stupid decisions like this one. I hated to send her into danger. I knew if one or both of us was caught, we would be in a bushel of trouble.

I pursed my lips, then grumbled, "Fine. When Peter goes to sleep, I'll sneak you to one of the tunnels."

217

Ella squealed. "Thank you, thank you, thank you!"

"Shhh."

When Peter came in, we all silently went to our beds. Ella and I had our backs facing each other, so I think she probably assumed I wouldn't be able to hear her sniffling through her tears. I turned over and held my cousin. Then, she cried freely until she fell asleep. Shortly before she did, I heard Peter's soft snores, so I knew he was asleep. I just laid there and stewed over the uncontrollable crisis.

I completely understood where Father was coming from with his orders for me to not be near the infected, with the quarantine, his meeting with the High General, and his brother being ill. I understood because I felt the same way. I felt the need to *do* something, anything to fix this for our people, but being next to helpless to accomplish that fix.

I would gladly even give up my life if it would save them.

"Psst. Do you think he's asleep?" Ella whispered. She must have woken up while I was musing. We paused to listen and Peter snorted loudly.

"Yes. He is," I whispered back. "Let's go."

Quietly, we got out of bed and walked over to the sliding door. When we made it to the hallway, I asked my Guard if he could get an extra Guard to help him since all three of us were sleeping in there tonight and he took off to do as I asked.

As soon as he was gone, I rushed Ella down to the third floor straight to the end of one of the guest halls. In one swift move, I flipped a picture on the wall and pressed the button to open the hatch that led to a secret stairway. I knew it emptied onto the field directly behind the palace.

"Be careful," I whispered as she began to descend the stairs. I closed the hatch and began to stroll back to my room. Just as I was approaching my room, I suddenly heard Ella screaming.

"No! Let me go!" she was saying.

I turned around and began descending the stairs to follow her.

"Don't bother, Miriam," I heard Father say coldly behind me.

Slowly, I turned around to face him. "Hello, Father."

He was glaring. "Are you insane, Miriam? What were you thinking? If she goes home, she could get what they have and die!" he yelled.

"Yes, sir. I know," I replied. "I told her that, but she insisted."

"If she asked you to buy her a light gun so she could shoot herself in the head, would you do that, too?"

"Of course not!"

"Exactly." He sighed. "Miriam, I think it would be a good idea for you two to stay in your rooms for a while. I need to be able to trust you. As future Queen, you need to realize that sometimes, decisions for safety need to be made regardless of whether or not it makes people happy."

He was right. I knew he was. I was ashamed of my weakness.

Am I really ready for all this?

"Yes, sir. I understand."

"Good. Am I also to understand that Peter is in your room sleeping right now?"

I winced. "Yes, sir. He is sleeping on a cot."

He pointed a stiff index finger at me. "Last night. Tomorrow, he is back to his own room. Understand?"

"Yes, sir."

As I made my way back up the stairs at the Core, I heard the front doors slide open. "Let me go! I demand to be let go! I need to see my family!" Ella was screaming and sobbing at the three Guards it took to control her; she was struggling quite a bit. They had resorted to actually carrying her around rather than trying to drag her. Her door would surely be locked from the outside when they got her in, as would mine.

"I'm sorry, Ella!" I shouted.

She stopped fighting for a moment and met my eyes. "You tried! I love you, Rose!"

"Love you, too!" At that point, the Guards rounded the corner to her room and I made it back to mine. When I opened the door, Peter was still snoring. I tilted my head and examined his peaceful countenance. With a sigh, I went back over to my bed and got in. As I closed my eyes, I realized this could be the last night I ever saw him asleep at peace like that.

Chapter 25

Early the next morning, I heard the chime ring on my door. I struggled out of bed and put on my robe before answering. After blinking a few times, I tried to open it. It only buzzed at me.

Right. Locked from the outside.

"Who is it?" I asked.

"It is the Steward, Princess. Count Lincoln of Elm is on the comm for you."

"Put him through," I said as Peter snorted loudly in the background. I shuffled over to my holostation and answered before it even beeped. Rubbing my eyes, I said, "What can I do for you at this ungodly hour, Linc?"

"I am so sorry to disturb you, Miriam. It is just – well, you see – Father told us about the disease and Mother has started showing symptoms."

I stopped rubbing my eyes and looked at him. "I am sorry, Linc. I am sure that is rough."

He nodded. "Leo, Christopher, and I have been talking. There are only four of us left. I know Peter is already at Evergreen Palace.

We think it may be a good idea for the three of us to come there, as well."

"The palace is on lock-down right now. No one comes in or out. Trust me. I just tried to smuggle Ella out so she could be with her family."

"Tried?"

"Unsuccessfully. All it did was get us locked into our individual rooms so neither of us would do anything else stupid."

He chuckled and I smiled. "Could you speak to the King about it?"

"I do not think he is going to budge and I do not think he would be very receptive to me right now. You may do better to talk to him directly."

Linc sighed. "I already did." He made a face that told me he was hiding something.

"What else is going on, Linc?"

"Well –although we are not showing any symptoms, Christopher, Leo, and I all tested positive for the disease." My face, I'm sure, turned pale as a ghost in winter. "I talked with your father about it; suggested that it would be best for us to be near Doctor Winston when he comes up with a cure, but he was insistent that the lock-down stay in place."

"I cannot believe all this is happening," I said as I covered my face with my hands. "I do not want you all to die."

Linc laughed dryly. "Neither do we."

I cupped my chin in the palms of my hands. "The only thing I can think to do is to talk directly with Doctor Winston. Perhaps *he* can convince Father it is for the best."

"Do you think he will listen to you?"

I shrugged. "Maybe. He and I have kind of become friends since all this began. I will give him a quick comm and let you know how it goes."

Before I could disconnect, Linc said, "Miriam?"

"Yes?"

"Thank you. It means a lot that you are doing everything you can for me. For us."

I smiled. "Of course, Linc."

After disconnecting with Linc, I put in the address to comm Darrel. As it beeped, I looked over at Peter, who was still sound asleep. He looked so at peace, as if nothing was wrong in Arboria. "Miriam?" Darrel said.

I looked back to the holocomm to find an exhausted Darrel. "Hello, Darrel. I have a favor to ask of you."

"What is it?" Darrel pinched the bridge of his nose and sighed in a way that told me he really couldn't take more work at the moment.

"I am sure you are aware that Count Brian of Birch and his family have died?"

"Yes."

"I got a call from Count Lincoln of Elm. He tried talking to Father, who was unreceptive, then me, but I could not do anything

223

for him. As I am sure you know, Count Christopher, Count Leonard, and Count Lincoln all tested positive for the disease. Given that there are only four participants for the King's Test left, he feels it is prudent, and I agree, that they be on premises for when you develop a cure for them."

Darrel sighed. "Miriam, I am doing my best. I am not feeling very encouraged right now. I keep thinking I am close, then another family dies." He paused and sighed again. "What I am trying to say is that it is more likely a case of *if* not *when* the next family will go."

"I understand, but if you *do* come up with something, would it not be best for them to be nearby? I would rather not imagine marrying a foreigner from the batch that has been selected. Prince George and Prince Xi Roger, I know, would be dreadful for Arboria, not to mention me."

Darrel bit his lip and seemed a bit shaken at my statement. "I suppose you are right. I will let the King know I need them to come here."

"Thank you, Darrel. Thank you, *so* much."

When Darrel disconnected, I commed Linc back and let him know the good news. He was very happy, but I could tell he was also scared and that he had a headache. He couldn't stop rubbing his temples the whole conversation.

After our discussion, I went back to bed. When I heard him sigh and yawn, I knew Peter was awake.

"Are you wanting to get up, Peter?" I asked.

Still yawning, he said, "Never. Go ahead and go to sleep. You seem tired. Long night?"

"You have no idea." Speaking with a yawn of my own, I said, "I'll tell you about it when I wake up. Love you."

"Love you, too. I'll never get tired of hearing you say that."

I smiled and went to sleep.

~ ~ ~

Opening my eyes, I stayed completely still. Peter was sitting in a chair reading. All I wanted to do was bask in the secure feeling of being in Peter's presence when waking. I didn't want it to end. Something told me this would never happen again. Even if he ended up being the last nobleman left and the King's Test was cancelled. I felt it deep in my soul that things would not end well.

I wasn't sure if I was being pessimistic, realistic, or what, but no matter what I told myself, I couldn't shake the feeling.

I turned around to find Peter wide awake and smiling. I smiled back, but apparently, it didn't reach my eyes because Peter noticed it was a little forced. "What's wrong, *Darling*?" He was teasing me about the other night when I called him that.

"Shut up, Peter." Then, I really did smile. "Aside from the unshaking feeling of impending doom, I had a bad night."

"I noticed you moved over here and Ella's gone. What happened?"

I giggled. "You are a hard sleeper. Did you know that?"

He laughed. "Yes. Mother used to tell me that all the time."

I fiddled with a stray string on the blanket we shared. "I tried to help Ella escape the lock-down last night and we got caught. We are both locked in our rooms until Father decides we're not going to do anything else stupid. I assume that means until Ella's family is all gone."

He frowned. "Are you insane?"

"Father asked me the same question. I just wanted to help Ella; to respect her wishes." I put my head on his chest and he began to stroke my hair.

"At least you had good motives."

"I wish Father would have seen it like that. Poor Ella. All alone at a time like this." I had an idea. "Peter, could you do me a humungous favor?"

Peter lifted both his brows. "Not if it's something stupid."

I laughed. "I don't think so. As much as I love having you with me, Ella needs someone more right now. Can you go be with her? Be the friend she needs right now? You're the only one who can understand what she is going through with her family."

Then, his brows furrowed. It was almost comical how different his face looked between raised brows and furrowed brows and I bit back a smile. "You would be alright with me being alone with another woman in her room?"

"It's not my *first* choice, but I trust both of you. And I believe in your love for me. And I know Ella needs someone right now."

Peter softened his expression and kissed me. "I love you. Alright. I'll get dressed and head right over there. I'll let her know you're thinking of her."

"Thank you, Peter. I love you, too. Now. Shut up and go." I smiled and he smiled back.

Chapter 26

In the following days, Peter spent most of his time comforting Ella. It took much longer for the Maples to succumb to the modified Daze than the other families thus far and Ella really did need someone. When he wasn't with Ella, he was delivering verbal messages between us – we had later discovered our addresses were blocked from each other on our holocomms. We were both angry with Father for keeping us apart when she needed me.

My time was mainly spent in very productive ways – including watching classic television and film, and reading classic literature from the twentieth and twenty-first centuries. I loved the old sci-fi shows, like Doctor Who and Star Trek, and fantasy books about girls becoming adults only to discover they are actually something different than they thought. Several books had characters involved in acting, something I always wished I could do, but never could because of my position. By reading and watching the holocomm, I managed to escape my room, if only in my mind.

While closed to the argument from Linc, and probably me, Father was open to bringing the three other Counts into Darrel's lab when Darrel spoke to him. When they arrived, I asked if I could go see them and Father immediately denied my request without argument, then disconnected the comm. Since he wouldn't let me go down, I commed Darrel and had him let the men know they were in my thoughts and I would visit them as soon as I could.

When my birthday was only a week away, Father finally released me from my room. He still wouldn't let me down to see Linc, Leo, or Christopher, but he said it was because he needed me down in his office and that I could visit when I was done with him.

As I hurriedly got dressed appropriately for a meeting with Father, I wondered what could be happening that he would release me from my imprisonment. I also wondered where in the world Marie was; I hadn't seen her in a few days. When I was ready to go, I tried to leave, but found my door still locked from the outside. My Guard let me out and escorted me down the spiral stairs around the Core.

When I opened the door to Father's office, I saw Marie sitting in a chair wearing magnecuffs and looking forlorn. Standing behind her was a gentleman I didn't know, but who was wearing the uniform of a detective with the Petrichorian City Guard.

I stopped just past entering and the door caught the hem of my wide leg trousers when it shut. "Father?" I tried to step forward, forgetting about my pant leg and frowned at it. Frustrated, I smashed the button so the door would slide open and strode in with false confidence.

"Father, what is going on here?"

"I was hoping you might be able to help me with that," Father replied sadly.

I looked at Marie, but she wouldn't meet my gaze. "Marie?" I said and she winced.

"Allow me to introduce myself," the stranger said. He seemed a bit smug, but all the detectives I ever had the displeasure of encountering were. "I am Lieutenant Hanson of the Petrichorian City Guard." He bowed. When he straightened, I nodded an acceptance of his respect.

"Very well. I will ask again. Father, Lieutenant, what is going on here?" I asked, beginning to get irritated that no one had yet answered me.

"Marie DeWittacker is a spy," Hanson said frankly.

I quirked an eyebrow in disbelief and looked between him and Father. With a dry chuckle, I said, "You cannot be serious. *Marie*? She is probably the most loyal person to me aside from my family and Peter." I looked to the woman who was still avoiding my gaze and noted her evading posture. The little humor I had left. "Marie? Please, tell me the Lieutenant is reading into some circumstantial evidence and it is not true." Lieutenant Hanson frowned, and she looked up at me with wet eyes.

"I am sorry, Miriam," she said and looked away from me again.

"Marie?! What?! Who are you spying for? Are you working with those responsible for the deaths of all those people? For *Stephan*?!" I asked. My head was spinning. I looked to the Lieutenant. "How – what?" I looked back to Marie. "Why?"

Marie still refused to look at me. "She is a part of a movement," Hanson began. "We do not know the name of it or its origins, but it is a new one. In a nutshell, they want all the Nobles dead so new common Arborians can move into their places."

"Is this true, Marie?" I asked her.

This time, she *did* look at me, her eyes wild and pleading. "Yes, it is true, Miriam; we want new Nobility. But we are not responsible for all those deaths. We are not the ones killing people. I promise. I would *never* put you through the pain of losing Stephan or anyone else you love."

Clouds covered my sight as I listened to her and I stumbled back across the room. "I cannot believe this. You were my friend. I trusted

229

you." I said quietly while I turned away from her and made my way to a plush chair.

"Do you have any evidence linking her to the deaths of the Nobles, Lieutenant?" I asked contemplatively.

He shifted on his feet. "That is not something I would like to discuss while the prisoner is in the room," the pompous Lieutenant answered.

"Then send her out!" I shouted. "Guard, take her outside the room while we discuss this. If she escapes, I will personally sign your dishonorable discharge. Am I understood?" The Guard I was pointing at nodded stiffly, only slightly showing his surprise at my outburst, and rushed to take her out of the room.

"I am not innocent of being a spy, Miriam, but I swear! I am *not* responsible for anyone dying!" Marie shouted as she was dragged from the room.

When she was gone, I pointed at the Lieutenant and commanded, "Speak. Now."

He frowned, but Father smiled at the way I took charge.

Good. Maybe he'll have a little more faith in me and respect for me now.

"We have nothing solid as far as her being connected to the deaths, but she is definitely responsible for giving these rebels information," Hanson said.

I shook my head. "I cannot believe this!" If something were within reach, it would have been sent flying across the room. "Have you discovered who she was speaking to?"

"Not yet, but we are running through her holocomm recordings to see who she has been speaking to and what she has been saying."

"Recordings?" I asked and looked to Father.

Father cleared his throat. "It is not something widely broadcast, but all communications to and from people on the palace staff are recorded. It is for security purposes."

I frowned at that. "That does not seem quite right. We really do not have a right to be invading their privacy like that."

"We will have that discussion another time, dear. Right now, let us discuss this. Has Marie seemed odd at all lately?" Father asked.

I thought about it and shook my head. "No. She has been as attentive as always. More so, even, with the emotional rollercoaster I have been on lately."

"How open are you with Marie?" Hanson asked.

"Very. I mean, I do not share *everything* with her, but when Countess Elleouise is not around, she is my confidant. However, any information she has garnered from me is personal in nature. I do not discuss Council meetings or anything of the sort."

"Nothing political at all?"

"Not beyond telling her I am stressed out of my mind about the King's Test and Crowning Coronation."

Father's door chimed and he pressed the button his desk to admit the new guest. A young woman walked over, whispered something to Lieutenant Hanson and he frowned. "I see. Thank you for letting me know," he muttered to her and she left.

"News on the case?" Father asked.

The case? This isn't a murder mystery, Father… Well… I guess it kind of is.

"Yes, Your Majesty," Hanson said. I hated how he treated Father with so much respect and talked to me like I was a narcissistic brat.

Princess Problems.

"It appears that my researchers have made quick work of Ms. DeWittacker's recordings. We have had several more arrests from right here within the palace." I shook my head in disbelief. "If you will excuse me, I have some more interviews to perform. I will let you know if I learn anything else."

Father stood to shake his hand. "Thank you, William."

Lieutenant Hanson bowed to me again and left. Father took his seat again.

"Man acts like he is the twenty-third century Sherlock Holmes," I muttered and lay my head back.

"Who?" Father asked.

"Oh. He was a fictional brilliant detective originally written in the nineteen century. His character's popularity only declined when the Daze hit and everyone became more concerned with reality than escaping from it with books or film."

"Huh." Father paused. "Are you alright, Rose?"

"No. No, not really." Tears had been slowly dripping down my cheeks since my eyes clouded over.

Father sighed. "I didn't know our people were so unhappy that they would kill all the Nobles."

I shook my head. "No. Marie could never – she wouldn't."

"She *did*. Even if she didn't know the people she was working for planned to do it, she still reported to them."

I looked at him and whined. "Why? I always treated her well. She gets paid better than most in the palace. I can't understand why she would betray me like this."

We sat together in reflective silence for some time. Marie had been with me for so long; nearly as long as I had known Peter. She had stayed up late with me several nights as I talked about my romantic meetings with Peter. She gave me advice when Ella and I had an argument. She looked through my picture books from the twentieth and twenty-first centuries. I had trusted her implicitly for years – and she was a spy.

Both of us were still moping when Darrel holocommed Father. "Your Majesty, I was calling to inform you that the Duke and Duchess of Elm are both dead and, the now, Duke Leonard and Count Lincoln are – not doing well. If Princess Miriam wants to see them, she had better come down now," Darrel said when the comm was connected.

"I don't feel comfortable with her visiting with them. I've already expressed to her I don't want her in your lab," Father said.

"It is not possible for her to get their mutations of the Daze. Each form is family specific. I promise she will be safe here," Darrel assured. Father hummed and looked over to me.

I buried my face in my hands and sighed into them. "Tell him I will be there soon," I mumbled through my hands. Father pressed his lips together, but relayed the message and disconnected the comm session.

"I don't like this and you know it," he said.

"Please not this again," I begged.

"But as you seem to be hell-bent on going down there, and I understand where you are coming from, I will allow it. I think Doctor Winston has provided enough evidence showing it's not transmutable outside of each family. Will you be alright?" he asked.

I laughed humorlessly. "We'll see." I stood up and made for the door. Hand hovering over the open button, I paused and considered telling him about my premonitions.

No. He wouldn't understand. And he would certainly reconsider the Crowning Coronation if he knew.

I pressed the button and left. The hall was empty. Marie, who I thought was my friend, was long gone and probably in a cell at the local jail now. I wondered what would become of her. I knew the punishment for treason and pushed the thought out of my mind.

When I got to Darrel's lab, I went straight to the quarantine rooms. Darrel was leaning against a wall with his feet crossed, pinching the bridge of his nose. I felt sorry for him, thinking it must be difficult to spend day and night trying to save people and having them die before he could do it.

I placed a hand on his shoulder and the hand on his nose moved on top of my hand. He knew who it was. "Are you alright, Darrel?"

He looked at me with wet eyes. "I cannot do it. There is nothing I can do. It is too late for all three at this point."

I removed my hand. "What do you mean? Has Christopher begun showing symptoms now, too?"

He nodded. "Perhaps. He is complaining of a headache. I just came from his room. I am going to try, Miriam, but – I have not experienced this much failure in my entire life." He paused for a

234

second. "I cannot stop thinking about your dream. I want you to know. I will not let you die."

His face held a mix of expressions I couldn't place. Friendship, definitely. Love, no. Determination, yes. The one that confused me was guilt. There was definitely guilt.

"Do you feel guilty for all those people dying, Darrel?"

His eyes widened as if he couldn't believe I sensed it. "How could I not?" He held his arm straight out toward the quarantine rooms. "All those people? Full families? They *depended* on me. *I* was supposed to rescue them. *Me.* I have friends all over the world working on it and even *they* cannot do it."

His last statement surprised me; I wasn't aware he had his colleagues helping him, or if he had permission to share the information with anyone, but I let it slide. I placed my hand on his shoulder again. "Darrel, it is not your fault. You are not the one who infected them all. You are doing all you can. No one blames you. No one."

Darrel let out a deep sigh. "Thank you, Miriam. I think you had better go in there now if you want to see Duke Leonard. I must warn you, though. His family's mutation created some pretty intense boils all over their bodies."

I nodded as he let me in, but his statement didn't truly prepare me for what I saw.

Poor Leo.

Slowly, I made my way over to the bed that he was strapped in. It was the same one Stephan had died in. I let the memory of his screaming face and bulging eyes enter my mind for only a moment. This was Leo's time.

"Leo?" I said as I sat on the edge of the bed next to him. He was sound asleep. Boils of all sizes covered his body and face. The largest was the size of a cherry tomato on his shoulder. He didn't stir, so I touched his face and said his name again.

His eyes lazily opened and his dry lips cracked in a way that looked painful as he smiled at me. "A beautiful sight to wake up to."

I smiled at him and took his hand. "You just can't help yourself, can you?"

"Nope." His face became serious. "I would have told you every chance I had. You know that? I would have written you songs and poems and romanced you into old age if I had ended up your husband." His face scrunched in grief and tears filled his eyes. "That was *always* more important than being King to me. I hope whoever *does* end up marrying you will treat you like I would have."

I tear escaped my eye just after one escaped his. He was truly concerned for my future well-being. Though I still thought he was a bit of a creep, he was a sweet creep; a sweet creep on his death bed and I would hear and accept whatever it was he felt like he needed to tell me before he died. It was literally the most I could do.

"Oh, Leo. Listen to you. There is no need to worry about me. I'll be alright."

"What will happen to you if all seven of us die? Will you get to choose a husband, then?"

I sighed and smiled sadly. "No. That was never a choice meant for me. I imagine we will have to do a King's Test with foreign participants or maybe I can convince Father to allow common Arborians to participate. I think I would rather the latter."

Leo smiled. "Me, too." He frowned in pain and crushed his eyes together for a moment before looking at me again. "Is it true that Peter has tested negative for the disease?"

I nodded.

"If he's the only one of us left, would he become King by default?"

"That's certainly one possibility."

He licked his dry lips. "Isn't that suspicious to you? I mean, I know he's been your friend for a long time, but – I don't know. Maybe I'm just jealous."

I sat back in my seat. "Maybe." But there was something to what he said. I hadn't considered it before because I was in love with Peter, but now that Leo had mentioned it, the seed of doubt had been planted.

"You're not sick, right?" Leo's question broke my thoughts.

"No. I'm not. But that doesn't mean I'm not scared of it happening. Poor Doctor Winston is beside himself with guilt over not being able to save any of you."

"I don't bla –" His sentence was interrupted by the sound of male screaming in the next room, Linc's room. "Linc," Leo croaked. "Go to him, please. And, please, don't come back. I am *so* glad you came, but I don't want you to see me like this anymore."

I nodded and gave him a small kiss on his dried lips. I had put some gloss on earlier and could tell it soothed him a little. "You should have done that first," he said and we heard another scream. "Goodbye, Miriam."

"Rose. Call me Rose," I said, remembering how disappointed he had been when I didn't give him permission to use it before.

He smiled and tears filled his eyes again. "Goodbye, Rose."

I quickly made my way out of the door and found the door to Linc's room ajar. Darrel was standing next to him and Linc was sobbing. I walked over and saw what was happening. Several boils on his arms and legs had burst open and he was bleeding profusely. Darrel was holding a syringe I assumed held some kind of pain reliever because Linc wasn't screaming anymore.

I walked right over to him and took his hands. He opened his red eyes and met my gaze. "Rose," he breathed. I had never told him to call me that, but he must have been delirious or he had imagined calling me it before.

"Hi, Linc," I said softly and glanced at Darrel.

Darrel leaned over to me and whispered in my ear, "Minutes." I knew what he meant. Darrel left the room.

Linc swallowed hard. His lips were dry, too. Taking Leo's advice, I leant over him and pressed my glossed lips softly on his parched ones. He let out a sigh of relief.

"I'm so sorry, Rose," Linc said.

"Whatever for?" I asked.

"For the tulips," he said, confirming my thought that he was delirious.

I smiled at him. "It's alright. I think tulips are beautiful, especially in the spring."

238

He was still looking me in the eyes. "But you love the roses, my sweet Rose of Petrichoria."

I smiled at him and dammed up the tears trying to escape my eyes. "Oh, but don't you know? Tulips are my second favorite. What do you say? When you get out of here, should we plant some in my garden?"

"I would love that. Is that a part of the Test?"

"No. This will be something special for us." I made a mental note to plant some tulips in my garden to remember these men who could have been my husband.

"Don't go into the coffin, please. It will hurt you."

My face blanched. "What did you say?" Eyes open, the image of the coffins came up again and the night man's silhouette kicked the wooden one off the end. I shook my head to bring myself back to reality. The migraine that hit me was the worst it had ever been and I struggled to maintain my composure.

Linc closed his eyes. "I think Leo is gone now."

"Me, too," I said, and meant it. "What were you saying about the coffin, Linc?"

Linc nodded. "The glass one."

"It will hurt me? Why would I go into a coffin if I'm not dead?"

"Not dead," he repeated. "Maybe 'hurt' is the wrong word."

"I don't understand." At that point, it occurred to me that I was trying to make sense of a delirious man's ramblings. However, the coincidence of his coffin imagery and my dreams could not be denied. It seemed as though he was having a lucid moment, though it could have seemed like incoherent nonsense to someone who didn't know better.

"Do you remember the fairytales with the sleeping princesses?" he asked and grimaced.

"Maybe you should stop talking, Linc. Maybe you should sleep."

"If I allow sleep, I won't wake up. I have to tell you this before I die."

I opened my mouth to say something, but he interrupted the action by continuing.

"Mainly the one about the Princess and the dwarfs who tried to save her? Remember?" I nodded. "Good. 'Hurt' is the wrong word. 'Change' is better. You'll sleep in that glass coffin. We'll be long dead when you wake and you'll be different."

"How do you know that, Linc?"

"I don't – know. I've – been having – these dreams. I – thought perhaps – I was crazy, but –I felt the need – to tell – you – that." His breathing was rapid and harsh, not allowing him more than a few words out at a time. "One – more – thing."

"I'm still here."

"Last words ever – please. Leave – when – I – say – them."

I nodded.

"I've – always – loved – you. I – love – you – still. I'll – love – you – even – in – death."

Obeying a man's last wish, I kissed him one more time and left. Darrel was in the hallway. I leaned against the wall and slid down to the floor, clutching my knees to my chest.

"That was very kind of you, Miriam. Being there for them."

I nodded, the action bringing a stinging pain to the top of my head.

"Duke Leonard is dead," he said.

"I know," I replied. "Linc knew when it happened, too."

Gah. My head.

Darrel furrowed his brows. "How?"

"Apparently, he has had premonitions, too. I don't know if he felt it or envisioned it, but he knew when he died."

"Did you know before he told you?"

"Yes. Every time one of the participants has died, I have had a vision of the room of coffins. The first came when I closed my eyes and kissed Theo on his forehead; one wooden coffin just disappeared.

"The second was after Stephan died. In my rose garden, when I closed my eyes on my sofa swing, another wooden coffin disappeared.

"The third happened the night before Brian died. I saw a silhouette of a man the color of the night sky with glittering stars. He circled the coffins, placed his hand on the wooden one at the end and it disappeared.

"The most recent was while I was in there with Linc. My eyes were open, but the image of the coffins covered my real vision. The silhouette kicked one of the wooden coffins off the stage."

I gasped as the same thing happened again. That time, though, the silhouette pushed the wooden coffin over and laughed maniacally and dancing around like an imp. Only one wooden coffin was left. I shook my head again and screamed at the shooting pain in my head.

"What? Did it happen again? Are you alright?" Darrel asked, spinning over and holding me steady by my shoulders.

I nodded. "Linc is gone, I think. The silhouette pushed another wooden coffin and laughed. Need something for this one." I pointed at my head.

"All that is green and good," Darrel said as he went into Linc's room, then immediately came back out nodding. "He is gone." Darrel walked right past me, went into his office, then came back with a pill for my head.

After swallowing it without water, I said, "I think I know what the glass coffin is, Darrel."

"What?"

"Linc had another vision that he told me before sending me out of his room. Based on what I heard, I think it is a cryogenic chamber." I looked up at him. "Is it possible that I am sick and you just have not detected it, yet?"

"It is highly unlikely. But I will listen to the room recording and think about it. Would it make you feel better if I took another sample, Miriam?"

I nodded. "How is Christopher?"

"He still only has a headache. I think he has a few more days before he succumbs to the disease."

My headache already subsiding, I stood up. "Alright, then, I think I will come back tomorrow to visit him. If you could let him know about Leo and Linc and let him know when I will be back, I would really appreciate it."

We walked out to the drawing chair in his lab and he took another sample. As I made my way back to the palace, I thought about Leo's suspicions of Peter.

Was that mad rambling or logical reasoning Linc was spouting?

Chapter 27

Going straight to the holostation in my office, I put in the contact information for Lieutenant Hanson that Father had given me on my way out of his office earlier. He didn't answer, so I left a message.

"Hello, Lieutenant. I had a thought; one I hate that I had. I would like to discuss it with you to make sure it is something you have already thought about and disregarded. Please contact me in my office as soon as you can."

Reconsidering what I was trying to do, I leaned back in my chair and covered my face in my hands. My office was the best place for me to go when I was feeling like I needed to be alone. Because I rarely occupied the room, there were never maids, butlers, or assistants waiting in there. No one ever sought me out there, either. The only company I had was a solitary Guard stationed outside the door, who I personally paid extra to stand there regardless whether or not I was in so it wouldn't give me away when I was.

Why am I about to put Peter under investigation – at the very least, suspicion – by the Petrichorian City Guard? What do I have to go on besides a dying man's paranoia? It's not like Peter has done anything to tie him to what's going on. He's certainly not smart enough to do it on his own. But he does *have charm and leadership potential. Could he be in charge of some kind of coup? Would he put me in a glass coffin? Could he be responsible for the death of his own family?*

I've only known him a little longer than I've known Marie. Marie, who I trusted. Am I a fool to trust Peter the way I do? No. I can't let what happened with Marie impact my relationships with everyone I know.

My door chiming interrupted my thoughts. I considered briefly if I should ignore whoever it is, so I didn't give away my location, but decided to allow them in. I pressed a button on my desk and the door slid open, allowing entrance for Lieutenant Hanson.

Ugh. I wanted him to comm, not come in. I should have ignored the door chime.

Lieutenant Hanson bowed and I greeted him. "Good afternoon, Lieutenant. Thank you for coming to see me. Please have a seat."

"Of course, Your Highness." He sat across from me. "I would like to apologize before we have any kind of conversation. I was extremely rude to you earlier concerning Ms. DeWittacker. I know it must have been difficult to find out about her treachery."

"All is forgiven, Lieutenant."

"You said in your message you had something you wished to discuss with me?"

"Yes. But I do not want it to be broadcast to everyone. I – It is difficult for me to even bring up, but after what happened with Marie this morning and after some suspicions I heard from Duke Leonard on his death bed –"

"Duke Leonard is dead, then?" he interrupted.

"Yes. And Count Lincoln." He nodded and I continued. "Anyway, he brought something up that I had not considered, probably because of my blindness to those I care about. At first, I took it as inconsequential ranting, due to the nature of the disease, but the more I think about it, the more I think it is possible. I only hope it is something you have already considered and dismissed.

"Are you aware that Count – I am sorry – Duke Peter of Juniper is the only male Noble who has been tested negative for any version of the mutated Daze?"

"Yes. And Duchess Elleouise of Maple is the only female Noble who has been tested negative."

"Right. My *light* suspicion lays on Peter, though. He has everything to gain by the other noblemen being gone. If he ends up being the only one left, it is quite possible he could become King by default, should the King and Council decide against hosting a different form of King's Test."

He nodded. "What about Countess Elleouise, Your Highness?"

"What of her?" I furrowed by brows.

"Certainly, you are still here *now*, but should you become infected and die, and without her parents living, would she not be next in line for the Crown?"

"I – Well – I had not thought of that, but I suppose you are right."

"And You, Duke Peter, and Duchess Elleouise are very close, yes?"

"Yes. However, Stephan was also very close to us."

"Yes, but if Stephan were alive, Peter would have to compete with him."

"I am not sure I understand what you are saying."

The Lieutenant propped his elbows on his knees and leaned his chin on his folded hands. "With all the noblemen gone and you out of the way, it would open the doors wide for Duke Peter and Duchess Elleouise to take the Crown."

My eyes widened. "You do not seriously think they would –"

"I do not know. That is why it is one among many theories we are exploring."

Could they do that to me?

I stood up and walked to the window, which faced the wide field of wild flowers that led to the forest. Biting my thumb nail, I considered everything the Lieutenant had just said.

Is it possible that my own flesh and blood would turn against me like that?

I shook my head. It didn't make sense; at least, I didn't want it to. In reality, it made perfect sense. Along with at least ten other theories I was sure the Lieutenant had been considering.

Not turning around, I asked, "Have you found any solid evidence indicating such a plot?"

"No, Your Highness. But I assure you, we are exploring *all* options."

The way he said it made me turn around to look at him. He averted my gaze. "I am a suspect, am I not?"

After hesitating, he said, "Yes, Your Highness."

248

I nodded. "My motive being my well-known distaste for the King's Test." It was a statement, not a question.

"Yes, Your Highness."

"Is there any way for me to clear myself? I will be glad to do whatever it takes because I have done nothing wrong. I have held the hands of three dying men and have made numerous trips to question and assist Doctor Winston."

When the Lieutenant turned a shade of red, I was sure he was angry with me, but his words and tone didn't match my assumption. "I understand that you have been going through a lot, Princess. You have had a friend die, a friend betray you, and you do not even know who you can trust anymore. If you will allow a search of your rooms and office, and access to your holocomms so we can listen to the recordings, it will be quicker to clear your name."

"Fine. Follow me." After he stood up, I grabbed his chair and dragged it over next to mine at my holostation. I expanded the viewport so the receiver would see both of us. "Put in the address to whoever I need to speak to." I sat hard – not plopped – into my seat, then gestured for him to sit back down in his chair.

Lieutenant Hanson smirked and took his seat, then typed in the address. "Detective Pleth," a young blonde woman answered the comm.

"Hello, Detective. This is Lieutenant Hanson. I need you to take a Statement of Allowance from Princess Miriam."

The young woman's big blue eyes widened as recognition seeped into her brain. I bit back a laugh. "Princess – Princess Miriam? Sir?"

249

"Yes, Detective. She would like her name cleared from the suspect list. You were paying attention during our briefing this morning, right?"

"Yes, sir. Of course, sir." Detective Pleth looked down and tapped on a screen that only she could see. "Alright, Princess Miriam. I am going to put up a transcript for you to read aloud. There will be a few blanks for you to fill in. I am obligated to tell you that this is recorded and action will be taken immediately following your Statement of Allowance. Until the investigation of your property is complete, you will not have access to it. This includes, but is not limited to your rooms and communication devices. Do you have any questions?"

"No, Detective Pleth." I glanced at the corner of the screen and realized I was late for dinner.

Oh, well. Just something else to top off the awesomeness that is today.

"Good." *tap. tap. tap.* "You should see it now, go ahead and begin when you are ready. Recording has already begun."

I sighed and looked at the words on the screen. "I, Princess Miriam Petrichoria of Arboria, give this Statement of Allowance to the Petrichorian City Guard to search my room, bathroom, and office and take what property is necessary, including, but not limited to, my holocomms so they can assess my viability as a suspect in case number PR569356. I understand these properties will be unavailable for me to access until such a time as my name is cleared."

Detective Pleth tapped her screen a few more times. "Thank you, Princess. Lieutenant Hanson will now escort you from your office." Detective Pleth disconnected and, true to her word, Lieutenant Hanson stood, politely offered his arm to me, helped me stand, and escorted me from my office.

Chapter 28

"Thank you, Princess. Both for your cooperation and for bringing your thoughts to my attention. I understand the decision to implicate Duke Peter and Duchess Elleouise could not have been an easy one to make and allowing us access to your property will help in the investigation. Unfortunately, it will probably be a few days until your spaces are available for you. We will try to have your room and bathroom done first; hopefully by the morning of your Birthday Ball in three days."

I groaned. "Is that really only three days away? I wonder if I can cancel it this year."

Lieutenant Hanson smirked again. "That is not something I can help you with, I am afraid. Have a good evening, Your Highness."

We walked silently to the Core together, then went our separate ways at the stairs. I was surprised to see a team of the PCG making their way to my office already and another behind me on the stairs heading up to my room.

At least they'll make quick work of it.

When I entered the Dining Hall, I noticed Ella and Peter sitting next to each other, deep in conversation with my parents. Before, their sitting together never would have bothered me, but given my

251

new thoughts of conspiracies, it hit me hard. I stopped at the end of the table and stared blankly at the scene before me. Mother was the first to notice I had come in.

"Oh! Rose! I didn't even hear you come in!" Mother said.

Everyone turned to look at me. Peter jumped from his seat and ran over, pulling me into his arms and kissing me. I was so shocked, I couldn't respond physically. When he pulled away, he was smiling hugely. "Peter?!" I said, aghast that he would do such a thing in front of everyone.

Peter shrugged and everyone laughed. "It's alright, Rose. I have had many man-to-man talks with your father over the last few days. We're good for another three whole days. I will not hide this anymore."

I glanced over at Father, whose eyes were twinkling. Mother's cheeks were a brilliant shade of red. Ella was laughing so hard, I thought she would fall from her seat.

No. Peter and Ella would never *hurt me.*

I gave Peter a peck. "Alright, then. Let's go sit. I'm not very hungry, so I'm not offended that you ate without me." I glanced at a waiter and without smiling, asked, "Could you bring me a glass of sparkling blackberry juice, please?" The waiter bowed and left to get it for me.

I sat down between Peter and Mother. Everyone had stopped grinning and laughing and all stared at me like I had grown leaves from my ears. "What?" I asked.

"Long day, Rose?" Ella asked as she took my hand. It was nice to have her back after being separated for so long.

I nodded. "Sorry to spoil the mood. I'm not sure if you have heard yet, but Leo and Linc died this afternoon. I was there for it."

Ella and Peter looked surprised, but Father and Mother did not. "Indeed," Father said. "I'm afraid the news is worse than that, though, dear. Duke Christopher is the only one left of his family. How was he faring when you saw him this afternoon, Rose?"

"I – I didn't see him. Leo and Linc died within minutes of each other. It was horrible; a different kind of horrible than with Stephan. They were covered in boils. Leo spoke romantically to me and wished me all the happiness in the world. Linc was delirious. By the time it was Christopher's turn, I couldn't do it.

"I'm sorry for my weakness, Father. I asked Dar – Doctor Winston if he thought he would still be alive tomorrow and he said he did. Christopher had only begun having headaches today. I'll see him tomorrow." I looked down at my glass, which had arrived during my report, ashamed with myself.

"There's nothing to apologize for, Rose. It's understandable," Father said.

I sighed. "Also, I gave the PCG a Statement of Allowance for my room, bathroom, and office, so I'll need to stay in a guest room and have some of our guest clothing brought to it for the next couple of days."

"What?!" Peter asked.

I shrugged. "Apparently, I was on the suspect list because I hate the King's Test." I took an unladylike gulp of juice. "I have nothing to hide, so I gave him the Statement of Allowance." I unceremoniously finished my beverage. "Another, please." The waiter took my empty glass and left to get me another.

"Are you crazy, Rose?" Peter said.

I leaned back in my seat and sighed again. "It's possible. I think I'm going to bed after my next glass."

"After your – Rose! You have people trying to press charges against you searching your rooms and you're worried about getting sleep?! Rotting roots! What am I going to do with you?" Peter ranted.

"Peter, calm down," Ella said.

"Yes, Peter. Calm down," I repeated. "There's nothing to worry about. The worst that will happen is that I'll be out of my room until the morning of my birthday. Breathe."

He did. Peter took several deep breaths. "I'm proud of you for allowing that, Rose. It's impressive that you have no fear of transparency," Father said. "I think your mother and I are going to go to bed. I'll have some clothes brought to your favorite guest suite." Father gave Ella a knowing look.

"Ah. Yes. I'll be going, too. To bed. Yes. Good night, Rose – and Peter," Ella stammered. All three of them stood and left single file. Peter was still glaring at me.

I pinched the bridge of my nose and accepted my second glass of sparkling juice with a sip. "What now, Peter?"

"You're hiding something."

I looked at him with a tired expression. "What could I be hiding? If I was hiding something, do you think I would have allowed two teams of the PCG into my private things?"

"No. Not hiding something legally. You're hiding something personally."

I swallowed hard and looked back down. "I don't know what you're talking about."

"Yes, you do. Look at yourself. You can't even look at me for more than a moment."

I rolled my eyes and looked at him. "Better?"

"No."

"I don't know what you want me to say," I countered, setting my glass down.

"I want you to be honest with me."

Finally, I snapped. "I'm scared, Peter!" I screamed at him and stood with clenched fists at my side. I was shaking. "Terrified! I have held the hands of three dying men and will do so tomorrow for a fourth! Marie betrayed me! *Marie*! Who else can't I trust? Now I find out that *I'm* suspect in the deaths of all those people. And my future is more uncertain than it ever has been. What's going to happen to me?" Tears were flowing from my eyes.

"At least I had an idea before. I knew I had seven possibilities for a husband and I knew them all at least a little bit personally. I knew I would be crowned in four days. I knew all of the Noble families. Now all of those things are uncertain. I can't be normal. I can't even sleep in my clothes or bathe in my own bathroom or sleep in my own bed tonight." With a heavy feeling of defeat, I resumed my seat next to Peter. "What kind of a Queen will I be?" I asked rhetorically in a whisper.

Peter said nothing and did nothing for a few moments. I thought he might just get up and walk out. Instead, he eventually took my hand and walked me down to the guest room he knew I favored. As we walked in, I glanced into the closet to find it lined with a guest wardrobe in my size. The door slid shut behind us and Peter whipped me around to face him.

"You will be a wonderful Queen. Do you know why?" he asked. I shook my head. "Because you will face all those uncertainties with your head held high. You will flow with the changes. You will accept your destiny no matter what it looks like. You will show your kingdom a strong and wise Queen, even if you are broken into a million billion pieces inside."

Not believing I was hearing all that from Peter's mouth, I gaped at him. I knew he believed in me, but he had never put it, or really anything else, so eloquently. His brown eyes were on fire with the fervor in which he spoke and he bore his teeth like a lion displaying his ferocity. It was the first time I could really imagine him being King.

"Now. This is what is going to happen, Rose. You're going to draw your own bath, dry yourself off, pick out your own rotting night clothes, and tuck yourself into bed. You will sleep off whatever depression-ridden squirrel has nested in your head and wake up the woman I know and love." At that, he gave me a peck on the mouth and left me standing there stunned, alone with my thoughts.

There is no way he would betray me.

Chapter 29

The next day, Father called for an urgent meeting of the Council, though everyone but Father, Peter, Ella, and I had to holocomm in because of the lockdown. With so many holocomms spread all over the place, I felt more like I was in a media room than the Council Chambers. Glancing at the corner of the nearest one, I noted that it was past 1:30 in the afternoon.

Before I went to the meeting, I had called Darrel to check in on Christopher. I still hadn't seen him and wanted to before his end. Darrel said he was progressing rapidly, but he didn't see him dying until well into the night. After a large exhalation of air, I had stood up from my *guest* holocomm in my *guest* room and left for the meeting wearing *guest* clothing.

Oh! The price of transparency! Princess Problems.

When I decided to give the Statement of Allowance, I had done it on a whim. By any means, I didn't regret the decision, but I hadn't thought about all the little things I was used to being taken away. My hair smelled of blackberries instead of roses.

Again. Princess Problems.

"Ladies and Gentlemen of the leadership of Arboria. I call this urgent session of the Council into order," Father began. Everyone looked somber. At the last meeting, the minority of provinces had lost their Nobles; now they were in the majority. Those who hadn't lost their Nobles only had one left. The Delegate from Alder had puffy eyes from recent tears; probably over Christopher.

"As you are all aware, whoever the attacker was has essentially succeeded at killing the innocent Noble families of Arboria. Though Duke Christopher is still with us, Doctor Winston does not anticipate him lasting through the night. Luckily, we still have Duke Peter of Juniper and Duchess Elleouise of Maple with us."

Ella teared a little, probably because the weight of taking her father's title just rested on her.

Father continued. "Though none of us in the Royal family have tested positive for the Daze mutation after several tests over the last few weeks, we will not feel confident that we are out of the woods until this fiend is apprehended.

"That being said, with the upcoming Birthday Ball for Princess Miriam and her Crowning Coronation, we will be lifting the lock-down on Evergreen Palace."

"Wait a moment. You are still having the Birthday Ball?" Delegate Birch asked incredulously.

Father opened his mouth to say something, but I interrupted him. "It is not actually something that we have discussed yet, Delegate. I was actually going to suggest cancelling the Birthday Ball, but proceeding with the Crowning Coronation."

Father smiled and nodded. "Yes. I think that is an excellent idea. Either way, the lock-down is going to be lifted, but we will increase security."

"What of the King's Test?" Delegate Elm asked.

After a pregnant pause, Father said, "I have not figured that out yet."

"There are three options as far as I can tell," I began and everyone looked at me. "First, we could leave everything as it is. Because Duke Peter is the last of the noblemen, he could become my husband, and, thus, Crown Prince of Arboria under this plan. Second, we could reach out to the countries we were previously in contact with and have a King's Test consisting of foreign participants and Duke Peter. Finally, we could do a King's Test consisting of common Arborians and Duke Peter."

"Why is Duke Peter included in all the options?" Delegate Maple asked.

"Because he is the last nobleman of Arboria, he should be included in all of our options. After all, the King's Test was meant to be done by our national noblemen. It would make no sense to cut him out of it," I responded.

Delegate Juniper cleared his throat. "How does Duke Peter feel about all this?"

Peter's eyes widened as everyone's gaze switched over to him. Now *he* cleared *his* throat. "Well, the events over the last few weeks have certainly been unprecedented. Never in the history of Arboria have we been struck by such a horrible weapon.

"Understandably, I know some of you may take this as a biased opinion, but I truly believe it is our best option. Right now, our great kingdom needs solidarity. Having a King's Test of foreigners could prove problematic because they will not necessarily be able to acclimate enough to provide for the current unique needs of our people. A King's Test for common Arborians is not a *bad* idea, but those men will be unknown by most of the people.

"I know Princess Miriam's first option is the best option. Not only do our people know and like me, but they are familiar with me and know that Princess Miriam and I have been friends for many years. Should we decide to go with that option, it will ease the minds of our people and reassure them that the leadership has their best interests at heart."

Impressed, Delegate Juniper nodded her head along with everyone else. I could barely breathe.

Is this really happening? Could something good *actually come out of this all?*

"What do you think, Your Majesty?" Delegate Juniper asked Father.

Father leaned back in his chair and sighed. Putting a blank expression on, I gave nothing away as far as how I was feeling. When I looked over to Peter and Ella, I noticed the same blank expressions on them; except Ella was also biting her cheek.

Nodding, Father said, "I agree with Duke Peter on all accounts. If it is agreeable to the Council, in my opinion, Duke Peter is the best option for becoming Crown Prince for Princess Miriam."

I was unsuccessful at quelling the small squeak of excitement that escaped my pressed lips. Luckily, Peter was the only one who heard it and he looked over at me with a smile.

"I move to accept Duke Peter of Juniper as future Crown Prince of Arboria," said Delegate Maple.

"Seconded," said Delegate Sequoia.

"All in favor?" Father asked.

Everyone said "Aye."

"All against?"

No one said "Nay."

"The 'Ayes' have it. Shortly following Princess Miriam's Crowning Coronation, Duke Peter of Juniper and she will be wed and he will become Crown Prince of Arboria. Upon Princess Miriam's ascension to Queen, Duke Peter will be crowned King of Arboria."

Everyone applauded and I saw smiles on faces that I hadn't seen smile since the King's Test Ball nearly a month before. My happiness was overflowing. For a moment, all the death and destruction of the last month was at the bottom of my list of things to think about. That so many people could be made happy with something I longed for and could actually do overwhelmed me.

With a smirk, Peter stood, walked over to me, and kissed me on the cheek, receiving whoops and hollers from the men on the Council. I'm sure I was as red as some of the roses in my garden and I smiled sheepishly as Peter made his way back to his seat.

"Alright. Alright. Order everyone," Father said. "I am glad at this reaction. Hopefully the people will be just as happy with this decision. I will keep everyone appraised on the situation with the mutated Daze. This urgent session of the Council is now adjourned."

One by one, the holocomms shut off as the Delegates disconnected. When the last one was off, Peter jumped out of his chair, making it fly behind him and smash into the wooden wall. He ran over to me and yanked me out of my chair, causing me to squeal. "Yes!" he shouted and lifted me in the air by my waist and spun us in circles. Ella and I were both giggling and Father had a self-satisfied smile on his face. "You're going to be my *wife*," Peter said as he lowered me and pulled me into an embrace.

I am going to be Duke Peter of Juniper's wife.

261

Part III

Chapter 30

"If you'll excuse us," Peter said as he gripped my hand and dragged my giggling self out of the Council Chamber. Swiftly, he pulled me out the doors and around to the field of wildflowers behind Evergreen Palace.

"The future Mrs. Peter Petrichoria of Arboria, are you as happy as I am?" Peter asked when we reached the tree line.

I laughed. "I'm pretty sure you're happier than a family of worms after the rain."

"Now *that's* a lovely mental picture."

Biting the corner of my bottom lip, I said, "I never dared to think this would happen. I never dared to hope, but here we are."

"Here we are," Peter whispered as he pulled me close and pressed his forehead against mine. "I'm going to get permission to leave Evergreen Palace when you head over to the lab."

My smile faded. "What do you mean? We just got engaged!"

He nodded. "I need to go to the Juniper estate and get my mother's ring for you. You will wear it, won't you?"

Tears filled my eyes. "Of course I will, Peter. When will you be back?"

"So sure your father will give me permission?" he asked with a twinkle in his eye. "I'll be there and back again; I won't be there overnight. I'll get the ring and come right back to you. I'll probably be home late tonight. I'll make sure to see you when I get back."

Before I could smile fully, Peter pressed his lips firmly against mine. His mouth danced with mine, stealing every breath from my lungs and causing my heart to race to a speed I had never experienced before. He groaned and I sighed when he pulled me as close as possible to him. Any space between us felt like a mile. Any moment apart felt like a year.

I couldn't imagine ever doubting that love. How could I have thought it wasn't real; that I was just some pretty face for him? Peter loved me in a way I knew no one else ever could. Finally, he stopped the kiss and we panted in our tight embrace.

"I must go now. And you must go see to Duke Christopher," Peter said.

"It doesn't bother you? My being with those men on their death beds?"

"Rose, you do realize that we all knew we would be participating in the King's Test from a very young age. We were all essentially trained to love you and only you. Sure, Christopher and Theo dated other women, but only to their parents' chagrin. When you sat with Stephan, Leo, and Linc when they were dying, you were their love; you were the one they had waited their whole lives to be with. I know you don't love them romantically, but your heart of compassion that extends to them is one of the reasons I love you so much. They would have died alone if not for you."

"Alright, then. Don't forget to come see me when you come home," I said.

"Home," Peter whispered.

We walked to the front of the palace together, then split. He went inside to organize his trip and I turned to the lab to visit with Christopher. I strolled into the lab, trying not to seem *too* happy, given all the circumstances. When I got in, Darrel was standing in the middle of the room with a crazed look on his face.

"Darrel?"

He looked over to me and his face softened.

"What is going on, Darrel?"

Darrel's face twisted again. "I have rotting had it!" he yelled and threw a test tube against the wall, shattering it into sand. "How could I do it? How?"

"I think you need to calm down, Darrel."

He scoffed. "Being calm did not save them. Being studious did not give me the knowledge I needed. Being connected did not get me the answers. I am a gigantic failure and a horrible man!" He threw another test tube. Then another.

I pressed myself against the wall and began to shuffle to the quarantine hall. "Well, I think I will just leave you to shattering your test tubes and go visit Duke Christopher."

"Don't bother." He sniffed. "He's dead. Just like all of them." He gestured to the waiting mortuary across the room, which was filled with the bodies of every member of the Noble families. "All dead. All my fault. All my rotting fault."

I had to let the news fly over me because Darrel wasn't finished with his tantrum. Instead of throwing it, he simply dropped the test tube from his hand on the floor. It crashed against his foot, which I just then realized was bare. A giant slash appeared on the top of his foot and he screamed in pain and began to weep.

Slowly, I approached him and took his hand. "Darrel, have a seat. I will help you get cleaned up."

He snapped his hand out of mine like a toddler throwing a tantrum and sat down on his examination table. "What do *you* know about cleaning up a wound like this? Psh. I will probably need the cut weaver."

I tried not to scoff at his childish behavior and words. "As brilliant as you are, I am sure you can direct me on how to use the larger cut weaver. I have been weaving my own cuts with a smaller one for years. As for cleaning a wound, it is basic first aid, Darrel. You do not have to be a child prodigy to know first aid. I may not be you, but I am not stupid."

I made my way over to the wall where his first aid kit was stationed. Opening the box, I pulled out a cloth with the cleansing liquid and found the cut weaver on the bottom of the box. Without looking, I grabbed a table cart and pulled it over to where Darrel was sitting.

While I set everything down, I asked, "Do you always smash your feet with test tubes when you are angry? It is very destructive behavior."

"No. Just when nine families all died in under a month while on my watch."

"You are always on the clock, Darrel. We have had this talk. It is not healthy." I poured some cleansing liquid onto the cloth and wiped at his foot, causing him to wince.

"I'm beginning to think you're right."

"The sooner you accept I am always right, the easier life will be for you."

He smiled crookedly. "Thank you, Miriam. I was very wrong about you."

"You are welcome, Darrel." I didn't want to press him for an explanation of what he meant by that. He was in a very fragile state of mind.

When the cut was clean, I examined the cut weaver. As it turned out, it wasn't difficult to use at all. It was similar to my small one. I only had to aim and pull the trigger. As I began to weave his skin back together, Darrel said, "Hey, you are not too bad at that. You have very steady hands."

"Surprised? You should not be. I play guitar and dance. I am very good with my hands." I smiled for a moment, then let it fall. "I am sorry I was not here."

"Why are you apologizing to me? You were the one who wanted to be here for him."

"Yes, I did. But not only for him." I finished up with the cut weaver and set it down. Darrel was looking at me, confused. "I wanted to be here for you, too."

"I do not understand."

"With each death, it was taking a toll on you. I knew when Christopher died, you could very well lose it. I was hoping to be here so you would not. I am sorry I was not here. I was clearly right."

"The sooner you accept that you are always right, the easier life will be for you."

269

I laughed.

"There is nothing to forgive, but if it will make you feel better, you have my forgiveness. I am sorry you had to see me like that. Not exactly the most professional moment of my life." After a moment of silence, he said, "You are much kinder and more considerate than I thought. Thank you for being here for me."

"Why don't you join us for dinner tonight, Darrel? You can sleep in a real bed tonight, either at home or in one of our guest rooms."

"You're inviting me to dine with the Royal family?" He sounded amazed.

"Oh, please. Are we really going to have the titles discussion again?"

"Yes – I mean – no, we do not need to have it again. Yes, I will join your family for dinner. It would be an honor."

"Should I arrange a room for you?"

"Yes, please. I – think I would enjoy a shower."

"I would like you to shower, too. It has been a while. I can tell." I winked and he laughed. "Dinner will be at 6:00. See you then, Darrel." I made my way to leave and stopped at the door. "Darrel?"

"Hmm?"

"Thank you for everything you did. I know you did all you could and I really respect you for the way you handled this situation." His eyes still held a level of guilt in them, but the rest of his face graciously accepted my praise.

Poor Darrel. How long will he make himself feel guilty about all this?

Chapter 31

At dinner, Father did his absolute best to make Darrel feel appreciated without actually discussing the disease. Mother, Ella, and I also tried to avoid the subject at all costs. There were really two conversations going on simultaneously. One was between Father and Darrel discussing future experiments and the other was between Mother and Ella discussing Ella's nonexistent love life.

I focused on my plate and tried to not miss Peter. I knew he would be home soon, ring in hand. I wondered what it would look like and if it would fit. I imagined walking down the aisle and how handsome he would look in his tuxedo and ceremonial cape.

"Is that right, Princess?" Darrel was talking to me. Looking up from my plate, I saw all four sets of eyes on me.

Rotting roots. I have no idea what the question was.

"Yes, Duke Peter and Princess Miriam are engaged," answered Ella, saving me. She probably knew where my head was.

"Well, congratulations. May your marriage be happy and Arboria continue to prosper under your reign in the future together." Darrel lifted his wine glass in a toast and we all did the same.

"Thank you, Doctor Winston," I said. "Duke Peter actually went to his estate to pick up his mother's ring for me. That is why he is not here right now."

"He did?!" Mother exclaimed with a half-moon smile on her face. "I was wondering where he went. Have you thought about your dress, Miriam?" Because Darrel was present, we were using formalities.

"Ever since I was seven years old, Mother." Everyone laughed.

"What about your announcement speech?" Father asked.

I choked on the sip of wine I had just swallowed. "I thought you were going to do that," I croaked. Ella grinned in amusement.

"I was," admitted Father. "However, I think it would be better if you did. I would like for you to draw something up discussing the cancellation of the Birthday Ball, the resumption of the Crowning Ceremony, and your upcoming nuptials. Have it ready by ten o'clock in the morning, please."

"Uh. Alright." Whatever his reasons were, his face told me further discussion would be fruitless.

"Ah. Look at the time. I am afraid I must be going to sleep. I have some cleaning and arranging to do in the morning and I must get some sleep before. Thank you for inviting me into the palace for dining and sleep. It is an absolute honor." Darrel stood, bowed, and left.

I faked a huge yawn. "Yes, I should go, too. Need to work on that speech and get some shut eye."

"Is that Rose-speak for 'I need to go to my room and await my true love's arrival with my ring?'" joked Ella.

I slapped her arm. "Of course not!" I exclaimed, but the smile on my face gave me away and everyone laughed again.

When I walked over to kiss Mother on the cheek, she took my hand. "Rose, I know this has been a terrible month for all of us, but I am *so* glad that you are going to be able to marry the man you love. I couldn't be happier for you."

"Thank you, Mother," I said as she released my hand and I kissed Father on the cheek.

"I'll see you all in the studio in the morning."

As I made my way to my guest room, I thought about everything that happened and about how relieved I was that it appeared to be over. That afternoon, Father, Mother, and I had our blood tested again and it all came back negative.

I also considered the fact that I didn't know that Christopher had died. It was strange. For the other five men, I had a vision of a wooden coffin disappearing or being kicked or thrown. With Christopher, nothing happened, not that I was complaining. After each vision, my migraine had returned ten-fold and I was tired of having them.

However, it was disturbing to me that a vision hadn't come to me. Not knowing if that meant more were going to die or if there was even any meaning behind it had given me goosebumps every time I pondered it.

When I got to the room, I nodded to the Guard who posted himself outside the door and went straight to the bathroom to take a bath with no rose oil.

More Princess Problems.

After my bath, I got myself ready again for the night. Father had offered to hire me a new assistant, but I wasn't ready yet. Marie's betrayal still sat heavy on my heart and I didn't feel up to training someone new yet. Still mentally constructing my speech, I sat in front of the mirror and brushed my hair.

Deciding against a manuscript speech, I began to rehearse out loud the different ways of saying what I wanted to say. I practiced in front of the mirror so I could choose gestures and facial expressions. After a while, I looked at the small clock by the bed and saw it was eleven o'clock. Yawning, I wondered how much longer Peter would be.

Feeling prepared for the morning, I sat on the sofa and picked up a book I had brought up from the library. Next thing I knew, I was waking up to the sound of the door chime. Looking at the clock again, I saw it read one o'clock.

Groaning, I went to the door and let Peter in. "Hello, love," I yawned. "I tried to stay awake. I really did."

Wordlessly, he smiled at my grogginess and pulled his mother's ring from his pocket. Made of white gold with tiny diamonds circling an emerald center stone, it was beautiful. Lifting my left hand, he placed the ring on my ring finger and kissed it.

"I love you, Rose. Get some sleep." He gave me a kiss, then left me standing there.

Smiling, I gawked at the ring and got myself tucked into the bed.

Mrs. Peter Petrichoria. King Peter and Queen Miriam. I like that.

Chapter 32

Two coffins sit on the platform and the man who looks like the night sky circles them. Deftly, he jumps on top of the wooden one and with one giant stomp, sends it into the ground. I am not sure how I know, since he has no face, but I know he has a malicious smile spread across it. He gently drags a finger along the edge of the glass coffin containing me.

"It'ssssss time," he hisses in a loud whisper.

Jolting awake, I grab my head. Out of all the migraines I had in the last month, this one was the worst. Dragging myself out of the guest bed, I made my way to the bathroom for one of my caplets, finding I was out. With a groan, I put on a robe and stumbled out the door barefoot.

The Guard gave me a questioning look. "Out of migraine medication," I said, still holding my head in my hands. "Need to go down to the lab and get some." He nodded and followed me out.

After the longest walk to the lab ever, I pressed the button to go in and discovered it was locked.

No biggy. I'll use my royal override code.

Father, Mother, and I each had our own override codes so we would always have access to any room in the palace or on the palace grounds. I squinted at the bright screen, which made the migraine worse, and pressed in my code. Leaving the Guard outside, I went in.

Inside, it was blessedly dark, but light enough. Because of the rising sun, I could see. The floor was still littered with broken glass from Darrel's tube throwing, so I had to carefully make my way around the room in my bare feet.

I opened the cupboard he got the migraine caplets from before, but they weren't there. Not knowing where I would find them, I began opening cupboards and moving things around. I would apologize later for ruining his hard-earned organization and offer to help put it back together. Darrel tended to be a little protective of the way things were in his lab, which was why he went through assistants quicker than the Princes of Britainnia filed complaints with anyone who dared breathe the wrong way around them. None of the assistants could stand his obsessive behaviors for longer than a week and he couldn't handle anyone not as obsessive as he was trying to assist him.

Giving up on the first cupboard, I moved on to the next, then the next. After about five cupboards, I was beginning to wonder if he was out, too. As I moved on to the sixth cupboard, I thought about the vision. For obvious reasons, the night man scared me. I was frustrated that I could never see his face.

Standing on the top step of the short ladder I had been pulling with me, I looked at the highest shelf and found something odd. It was a line of empty syringes, but the last one was labeled "Miriam" and had a transparent purple liquid in it.

I wonder if he has developed something more permanent for my migraines.

I pulled down the syringe case and set it on the counter so I could get a better look. While I thought it was a single line of them from the ladder, there were actually several rows. Pushing the ladder out of the way, I bent over and squinted at the labels on the other empty syringes. There was a date on the case that was several months prior.

Oak. Oak. Oak. Oak. Maple. Maple. Elleouise. Maple. Willow. Willow. Willow. Willow. Willow. Willow. Willow. Willow. These must be from the vaccinations we got a few months ago for that disease Darrel said was making its way toward us. I remember thinking that was the largest syringe I had ever seen

I moved on to the last row of abnormally large syringes.

Royal. Royal. Royal. Miriam. Why is there one with my name on it? I already had the vaccine and it wasn't purple.

My eyes widened with realization. And I slowly backed away from the counter.

No. No, no, no. It can't be.

When I turned to run out the door, I was stopped by two strong hands grabbing my upper arms. Shocked, I stared with horror into Darrel's face.

"You weren't supposed to find that, Miriam," he said.

"Explain. Please tell me that it isn't what I think it is," I begged.

Darrel pressed his lips into a straight line. "I can't tell you what you want to hear."

"I trusted you! I was there for you over the last month and now I find a syringe with my name on it? Is it the Daze?"

Darrel sighed. "It is. Only your variant is a more proper version of the Daze. It would make the Rose of Petrichoria a poison to her people. I had decided not to give it to you since you proved yourself so different than I thought, but you found that. Now, I have no choice."

At that, I lifted my hands between his arms and pushed out, breaking his grip on my arms. Turning around, I tried to get away, but he was too quick. As soon as we separated, he brought his hands in front of himself and pushed my back, making me land hard, hands-down, against the counter.

I quickly grabbed an empty syringe and filled it with air. Turning around, I tried to stab him in the neck with it, but he stopped my hand with his and grabbed for the purple syringe with my name on it. I grabbed his hand and pushed back, stopping him.

"You may not know your science, but you're stronger than you look," he admired with a grunt.

Squeaking, I replied, "You don't have to do this Darrel. Please." His hand moved an inch closer to me and I squeaked again.

"Yes, I do. You have no idea what I've been through trying to get all this off without a hitch. As much as I appreciated your emotional support, you made the whole thing twice as hard with all your meddling."

"I thought you were my friend!" I was able to get a little closer to his neck with my empty syringe.

Darrel scoffed. "Friend. As far as I'm concerned, we only just became friends. All the Nobility ever did for me was mock and tease me. I'm a genius! A genius! And all I ever got was disdain." He pressed a little closer and I screamed. I heard the Guard outside trying to get in. "Be a good girl and take your shot now, Miriam."

"No!" I screamed and got closer with mine, but he got closer, too. His needle was now pressed against my skin, but not breaking it, yet. I squeaked.

"How did you know that shooting air into my veins with a syringe this large will kill me? I thought you were terrible with science." He was trying to distract me.

"Princess! Princess! Are you alright?" the Guard was yelling for me.

"I won't let you hurt anyone else," I replied to him.

"Oh. You've figured it out then? Yes. This was all a big experiment for me. I'm bringing the Daze back, then I'll cure it and *I* will be King. If you're a good girl, I'll cure you first. Since you will be the first carrier, it only seems right. I might even let you be my Queen."

Knowing I couldn't let that happen and he was about to inject me, I decided to do something crazy. The vision was right. It *was* my time. Even if I was going to die, I couldn't let him live and destroy what my ancestors worked so hard to build.

After releasing his hand, he fell forward. Even though he did inject me with the Daze, I got him with the air, too. When he fell forward, he had fallen right onto it. His eyes bulged and he choked, dropping his, now empty, syringe.

I pushed him down to the ground, pulled out the syringe and refilled it with air. Straddling his chest and holding his hands down with my feet, I stabbed him in the neck with it again. I repeated the process over and over until he was dead.

I heard murmuring outside the door. "No! Don't come in!" I shouted as I heard the beeping of a code being pushed in. I jumped off Darrel and ran for the door. The beeping stopped. "Darrel

Winston was behind the deaths. He was trying to bring back the Daze. He – he – he injected me with it. I'm contagious. I'm going back to a quarantine room. Get another doctor, get the lab cleaned before letting anyone in."

Silence fell between us and I was panting. I already had a migraine and now my head was easily ten times worse.

"Yes, Your Highness," one Guard said. "You stay here. Don't let anyone in."

"Yes, sir," said another Guard.

I locked myself up in a quarantine room, laid down on the bed where both Stephan and Leo had died, and wept.

Chapter 33

"Princess?" I woke to someone questioning me. Turning over and sitting up, I saw a man I was unfamiliar with, talking through a speaker in the room. "I am Doctor Mage. How are you feeling?"

"Horrible. I already had a migraine *before* he injected me," I answered.

The man nodded. He was older and had brown eyes, but that was really all I could see past his protective suit and mask. Not a fraction of an inch of his skin was exposed. In fact, the half-inch thick material was obviously designed more for safety than functionality because he had difficulties moving to do his work. There must have been some kind of connection between the suit and the speakers so he could communicate with me. "I still need to take some blood from you, but my team was able to test the air in here."

"And?"

"From what we can tell, it is some form of the Daze. Not the original, but not what the Nobility had either. This one is contagious. He only needed to inject you with it. We gas cleaned the interior, as you suggested, so everyone outside the lab is fine."

"Good. Could you let the King know he needs to get the security footage over to Lieutenant Hanson, so he can close his case?"

"Yes, Your Highness."

After a pause, I asked, "What happens to me now?"

"Your Father, Mother, and I discussed it. Ultimately, it is your decision, but we all think it would be best to put you in a cryogenic chamber until we can come up with a cure for you."

My glass coffin.

"How long do you think that will take?"

"Unknown. It could be days, weeks, months, or even years. We have no idea what exactly Doctor Winston developed. As far as we can find, the only injection was the one he gave you and we have not found any cure or information about a cure on his Computer Desk."

I gulped. "Years?"

He looked down. "It is a possibility."

I looked down to the ring Peter had given me only that morning. I liked the way it looked on my finger. Blinking, tears began to fall; all my hopes and dreams escaped me with them. Removing the ring, I handed it to Doctor Mage. "If you could tell Peter something for me, I would appreciate it. Tell him, he can do what he will with the ring. He can wait for me or he can move on."

The doctor nodded slowly. "So, you will go into cryogenic freeze?"

"Yes. Can I talk with Father and Mother before?"

"I will bring you in a holocomm and you can talk to whoever you want. I will have a cryogenic chamber in here in about an hour."

After he was gone, I sat on the edge of the bed and stared lamely at my blank finger. For less than a day, I had everything I needed and wanted. Peter and I were going to spend the rest of our lives together, but I couldn't expect him to wait years for me. It wasn't fair for him.

A short time later, the doctor returned and set up a makeshift holocomm station for me. "I will go speak with your parents and they will comm you when I am done. I will see you in around an hour, Princess."

"Alright." It was all I could say. I felt numb – well, besides my splitting headache. He left again and I was on my own. I thought of poor Peter when the doctor gave him the ring. I hated that I couldn't save myself better, but at least I could protect my people from the Daze. I wouldn't allow myself to go out among them in my condition. Or risk going out there while in a Daze episode. Or leave Arboria without an heir to the Crown. No. It was best for me to go into the cryogenic freeze and let the doctors do their work.

The holocomm beeped and I went over to the holostation. After a deep breath, I answered. Rather than Father or Mother, it was Peter's face I saw. "Peter."

"Yes. It's me. I – I got the ring – and your message," he said sadly.

"Please, understand, Peter. I love you and want to spend the rest of my life with you, but I could be in the cryogenic freeze for years. I don't feel like it would be fair for me to expect you to wait for me."

"I understand. I would feel the same way, but I want you to know something. I will wait as long as possible. I love you," his voice cracked and he cleared his throat. "I love you and want to spend the rest of my life with you."

"I love you, too, Peter."

"Uh. Ella – wants to talk with you."

His image disappeared and Ella's replaced it a moment later. "Oh, Rose! I knew I had a bad feeling about Doctor Winston! Are you alright? Of course you're not alright. What a stupid question. Do you need anything?"

I couldn't help but smile at Ella's rambling. "No. I'll be in the cryogenic chamber in around an hour."

"You'll come out. I know you will. I can't be Queen, Miriam. That's what *you* are meant for. You'll be awake before you know it."

I shook my head. "No. I have a feeling I won't – and I think I might come out the other side very different, Ella. Promise me that you'll be there when I come home. Will you?"

"I'll be here – and I'll make rotting roots sure Peter is here, too."

"I'll be here, Rose of Petrichoria!" I heard Peter shout in the background and we all laughed.

"Aunt Amoura wants to talk with you," Ella said.

Ella's image disappeared and Mother's came up in its place. "Rose," she whimpered. "My little Rose bud."

I smiled encouragingly for her. "Everything will be fine, Mother. I'm sure the doctors are already working towards a cure."

"Always thinking of others, even when you're the one suffering. Do you hurt?"

"Yes," I replied honestly. "My head hurts a lot, but I'm not delusional yet, so – there's that."

"You're going to miss your birthday."

286

"We can celebrate it when I wake up."

"And your Crowning Coronation."

"We can do that when I wake up, too."

"And your wedding."

"Well, there's nothing to be done about that. I don't want you guilting Peter into waiting for me for decades either, alright?"

Mother frowned and bit her lip, which told me that was exactly what she was planning. "Alright." She glanced up and to her left. "Your father wants to speak with you."

Mother disappeared and Father appeared. "I'm proud of you, Rose," he said.

"Why?"

"You thought before you acted. You didn't let those Guards in and you gave clear and concise instructions during an emergency. It makes you a hero in my book. You could have panicked and allowed the Daze to escape the lab."

"Thank you, Father."

"You will make a *great* Queen someday."

"Thank you, Father."

"Rose?"

"Yes?"

"I love you."

"I love you, too."

"We're going to give you some more time with Peter, alone this time. I'll see you when you wake."

"Bye."

A moment later, Peter was up again. His eyes were full of tears that he was no longer holding back. As I was opening my mouth to speak, the door to the quarantine room slid open and Doctor Mage pushed in a cryogenic chamber.

"I thought I had an hour," I said. Peter's brow furrowed and more tears fell down his face.

"I did not realize there was one here. I am getting it set up. It should not take long. I am pretty much ready when you are."

I swallowed and turned my attention back to Peter while the doctor set everything up.

"Peter, I'm scared," I said.

"I know. Me, too," Peter replied.

I chuckled breathily. "That's not very comforting."

"Neither are you," he said and laughed dryly at his own joke. "Ella's right, you know."

"What? That she shouldn't be Queen? I know she hasn't had the training, but –"

"Don't do that," Peter pled.

"What?"

"Make light of this. There is nothing light about this."

"I know. I just hate seeing you so sad."

288

"I wish I could kiss you one more time. I wish I had said and done a thousand other things when I saw you this morning. Had I known this would happen, I would have done things differently."

"True tragedy is never expected, my love. That's why we have to live every moment as if tragedy is right around the corner. I love you."

"I love you, too."

"Princess," Doctor Mage said and waited for me to look at him. "I am ready when you are."

"Alright, Doctor." I looked back at Peter. "I'm going to go to sleep now, Peter. I'll see you when I wake up."

"I love you."

"I love you, too."

"I'll be here." He disconnected.

Feeling empty, I turned in my seat and made my way over. I looked at the glass door to the chamber and ran my fingers along the edge like the night man had in my vision. Laying down, it did look a lot like a coffin. After climbing in, I nodded at Doctor Mage and said, "It's time."

Epilogue

I woke up with a start the first day of college. Sitting up, I brought both hands up to my head to run my fingers through my hair.

"Ew," I grumbled to myself when I realized my hair was dripping with sweat. In fact, I was dripping with sweat from head to toe. With a deep sigh, I turned, stood up, and involuntarily stretched. Why I was so stiff, I had no idea. It wasn't like I had done anything strenuous the day before.

I looked over at the clock and groaned when I saw that it was only 4:00 AM; my first course wasn't until 10:00. I tore the drenched sheets off my bed and tossed them into the laundry basket.

Better shower before I handle the clean ones.

Grabbing my hot pink bath sheet and a change of clothes, I strode to the community bathroom for my floor in my dormitory. My bare feet slapped on the cold tile floor; I knew I should wear some sort of shoes, but didn't care at the moment, considering the early hour.

"Miriam? Did you have that nightmare again? You look horrible." Said my friend, Megan. She must have heard my door open and shut. She knew I had been having this nightmare for weeks, even before I arrived there for school.

I glanced over to the mirror and noted that I, indeed, did look horrible. Tight lipped, I muttered, "Gee. Thanks. Yeah I had it again." She walked over to me and took hold of one of my cold, trembling hands and rubbed it between her nice, warm ones; I hadn't even realized I was shaking.

Eyes watching her working hands, she said, "It was really bad this time, huh? I've never seen you this bad. I mean, you're terrified. Maybe you should see the school therapist. That's what she's there for."

As she switched hands, I shook my head about the therapist. I didn't need a shrink. "It was pretty bad this time, but I really don't want to see a therapist. I don't think it would make any difference and I don't want to share my nightmare with a total stranger."

She looked me in the eyes and said, "Promise me you'll at least think about it."

"I promise," I lied. No way was a going to see a therapist. My recurring nightmare was probably just a result of everything I had been through.

She nodded her head, then left. After preheating the water, I stripped down and hopped into the shower. Closing my eyes, I recounted and tried to make sense of this dream for the millionth time.

I walk down the street in Seattle toward the Puget Sound and look around. Fear is in everyone's eyes, but I don't know why. For the first bit, I see people holding their hands to their heads, like they have a headache. As I stroll, the headaches seem to get worse until people suddenly stop. I do as well and notice everyone *around me has stopped moving.*

292

I walk over to a woman about my age and observe her. I am expecting a blank expression with still eyes, but what I see are her eyes open and shaking, like she's dreaming. She "looks" up and mimes that her hand was wrapped around something. She tugs and brings whatever she's seeing to her mouth and takes a bite out of it. She has a look of pure happiness as she chews as if it's the best thing she's ever eaten. Her eyes widen like she's scared and I back away, but it doesn't matter, she turns and runs off straight into the street. "Wait! The cars!" I scream, but she doesn't hear me. She runs straight into a moving bus and it doesn't stop moving. I gasp and bring my hand up to my mouth in an attempt to prevent vomiting.

I turn around and begin running toward the water. The people around me are all waking up and acting bizarre and deadly. They are all dreaming the same way the woman was and doing horrific things. One man draws a knife and tackles an old woman to the ground and stabs her. A woman jumps off her balcony and barely misses me as I pass by. I pick up my speed as a car runs into a lamp post. I finally reach the port and there are numerous people jumping off the side, following the people in front of them like lemmings.

I turn around and look at my beautiful Emerald City and see the chaos that has erupted from seemingly nowhere. The Needle is on fire, lights are flickering, screams echo from every direction. Then the lights go out. The sky is cloudy, so everything is pitch black. The screaming continues, but now the fire is out along with the lights. I can hear my rapid breathing and heart beat ringing in my ears, then a giant crunch above me. The overpass cracks down the center, I lift my hands in reflex, and then...

I wake up. Sighing, I finished rinsing the conditioner of my hair. I don't know what the dream means or if it even means anything at all, but either way, it's disturbing. I don't want to see a therapist. I don't want to know what my dream means.

293

Acknowledgements

First, and foremost, I would like to thank God for everything He has done for me. Most specifically, I thank Him for His inspiration and gift of writing.

I would not have been able to the Rose of Petrichoria series, without the support of my family at The Barn. Thank you for all your encouragement and love! My husband, Nick, was gracious enough to let me use his idea of the Daze for the pandemic in this series.

Several people read through and critiqued Dazed and I am appreciative for all of you, too: Julie Hauenstein, Lynnette Bonner, Sheri Mast, Becky Luna, Deborah Wyatt, Cara Koch, Rachel Custer, and Vanessa Thalhofer.

Note From The Author

Forgetting your life, or knowing someone who has, is a horrible experience. In 2007, my mother suffered strokes while recovering from quadruple bypass heart surgery. One of the debilitating consequences was a loss of short-term memory. Over time, her vascular dementia progressed to the point that she most often didn't remember most long-term memories either. On November 27, 2017, my mother, Judith LeFebvre Gosvener, was brought out of her illness here on Earth to blessed wholeness in Heaven

If you have a loved one who is living with dementia, it is understandable that it would be difficult to see them go through it, or even to experience the heartbreak when they don't recognize you. People with dementia don't have the luxury of remembering your last visit. They live in the here and now. While it may be hard for you to see them, give them the love and respect they continue to deserve because they are still human beings with human feelings.

They have forgotten, do not forget them.

About The Author

Katie Hauenstein was educated at Northwest University in Kirkland, Washington, where she met and married her husband, Nick Hauenstein. After graduating with her Bachelor's Degree in Communication, she had her daughter, Mary, and began writing her stories. Forgotten, the first book in the Rose of Petrichoria series, is her first published novel.

In her spare time, you can find Katie binge watching superhero/sci-fi/fantasy shows on Netflix, fangirling about Doctor Who, attending a variety of movies at the local theater, or with her nose in a book. She also enjoys cake decorating, online shopping, and other introverted activities.

Made in the USA
San Bernardino, CA
23 December 2018